ANOTHER TWIST

IN THE TALE

Also by
Catherine Bruton:

No Ballet Shoes in Syria

ANOTHER TWIST IN THE TALE

CATHERINE BRUTON

nosy
crow

First published in the UK in 2020 by Nosy Crow Ltd
The Crow's Nest, 14 Baden Place
Crosby Row, London, SE1 1YW

www.nosycrow.com

ISBN: 978 1 78800 5 999

A CIP catalogue record for this book is available from the British Library.

Printed and bound in Great Britain by Clays Ltd, Elcograf S.p.A.
Typeset by Tiger Media

Papers used by Nosy Crow are made from
wood grown in sustainable forests.

For my wonderful GCSE Class 2018-2020

Matt B, Oscar, Helen, Ben F, Tabby, Ben G,
Nia, Theo, Evie, Angus, Finley, Emily, Matt M,
Adrian, Filip, Ella, Joel, Wilf, Josh

"They were Hard Times, but ever the best of times!"

C.B.

Chapter 1

*In which we examine the worth of girls and
introduce the other Twist in this tale*

Girls! The female of the species. The fairer, the gentler ... some say the weaker sex. Girls, young ladies, little women: call them what you will, but in this England of 1828 – where our tale begins the melancholy fact remains that girls are considered not worthless but most certainly worth *less* than their brothers and fathers and sons and nephews. In short, girls are worth less than boys!

Worth less, how? I hear you ask. Why, quite simply in pounds, shillings and pence. When we calculate what it costs to feed and clothe a female child, particularly of the orphan variety (though gruel and rags be all they are fit for) versus the revenue said girls might yield when – or if – they are fully grown (for many orphans have

1

the temerity to die before they have repaid their debt to a society that has contrived to starve them to the grave!) it seems, alas, that employers will pay more for a boy apprentice than they will for a girl. The parish may sell on girl orphans as maidservants or kitchen wenches, but their wages over a lifetime are paltry compared to that earned by their menfolk. Yes, the facts and figures are incontestable: girls are – all in all – worth a great deal less than boys.

And it is this very circumstance that leads to the twist in our tale. Or perhaps I should say the *other* twist, for indeed there were two: one boy, one girl. My dear reader, you have no doubt heard the tale of Master Oliver Twist: that rags-to-riches Cinderella-boy, the parish orphan who became heir to the Brownlow fortune. But what few know – indeed there are only two on this earth who know the truth – was that the very night when that unfortunate woman birthed young Oliver, she brought forth first a girl babe into this unfeeling world. A second Twist, or really a first – ahead of her brother in every way – for young Miss Twist came out screaming and lusty, hale and hearty.

"'Tis a girl!" declared the midwife of the Mudfog workhouse, a wretched being named Old Sal, who took a sip from a small green bottle and rolled her eyes as she beheld the child. "Lawks, a-mercy, 'tis a crying shame! Waste of all that effort, ask me!"

Then that good woman set the girl aside on a little flock mattress, and focused her attention on the puling, mewling, kitten-like creature that was to be Master Oliver Twist.

"A boy, sir!" she declared when Oliver – after some moments of apparent uncertainty – gave forth his first sickly cry. "But a weakly one. Not like to survive, you ask me!"

"Did I ask you? Did I?" blustered the beadle who was in attendance – a corpulent, red-faced gentleman whose waistcoat was cut a little too meanly for his splendidly mountainous belly. "A girl *and* a boy! Two little burdens on the parish purse! What was this reckless young woman thinking?"

Alas, the thoughts of the reckless young woman, now mother to twins, we shall never know as – having whispered her last desperate words to Old Sal the midwife and pressed some items that will be of significance later in this story into that old crone's hands – she let out a last gasp in this world and expired.

"Why, the boy might fetch a sum as an apprentice but as for the *female*." The beadle – whose name I should here record was Mr Bumble – paused and sniffed the air like he was nosing out a good wine. "I fear we must allow Mother Nature to take care of her."

At this Old Sal – who had been more affected by the last confession of the young mother than the contents of her green bottle were able to overcome – looked up in alarm. "Bu' she's a lusty one, Misser Bumble! 'Tis a shame, so it be!"

For she knew what Mr Bumble meant by "Mother Nature's care". It was the same "care" the workhouse authorities administered to unwanted kittens and the kitchen dog's pups, who were tied in a sack and thrown in the canal for the good Lord to "take care on 'em".

"The last thing this world needs is another squawking female!" blustered Mr Bumble, wheezily standing over Oliver's deceased mother, a delicate-looking creature with translucent skin and large cornflower-blue eyes, now closed forever. "We'll take the boy to the cottage orphanage and see what we can make of him, but the other one – the *girl*…" He pronounced the phrase as if the very vowels were sulphurous. "Let me hear no more of her."

And so it was that on that snowy night in the town of Mudfog, some distance south of the great city of London itself, the other Twist in our tale found herself dumped a little way down by the riverside on a rubbish heap in the snow – a bundle of white rags containing a tiny twist of paper, and a red and screaming infant.

But nobody had informed young Mistress Twist of the prevailing wisdom on the worthlessness of girls. She had not been made aware that young ladies should be seen and not heard, nor that they deserved neither to be fed, nor listened to. And so this particular young lady demanded to be not only heard but fed – and fed right now.

And thus it was that several good citizens of the parish encountered her – passing by the screaming bundle with upturned noses and exclamations on the loose morals of mothers who abandon their offspring to lie screaming in the snow.

And so young Mistress Twist might have ended her days – and this tale – had she not been found by a young lady by the name of Baggage Jones.

Chapter 2

*In which we are introduced to Miss Baggage Jones
and find that the worth of a person is not always
measured in pounds, shillings and pence*

Baggage had not always been this young lady's
name. Indeed she was quite sure she'd had
another name once – but it was long buried in the hazy
memories of her fourteen years on earth, for whoever
had given it to her had not hung around long enough
to impress more than a dim recollection of a sweet
face and a soft smile upon young Baggage's memory.
And so her name had been lost, like a penny down the
floorboards, or an odd sock in the laundry – or suchlike items that seem quite set upon being mislaid. Over
the years, this young lady had become so accustomed
to hearing herself addressed thus – "Get over 'ere, you
baggage… Fetch this, you useless baggage… Get on,
you baggage, you" – that she had come to believe that

Baggage was indeed her name. She had added the surname Jones, being the name of her mistress, which she believed lent a certain elegance and gave her a sense of belonging – to someone at least.

And to be sure Baggage suited her name – as our names come to suit us, or perhaps we them (as sometimes people say our dogs do). For Baggage Jones was a scrawny scrap of a creature with a round flat face, rather crumpled and pale. She had been born with a harelip, and one eyelid drooped a little, the result of an overenthusiastic beating with a wooden spoon (which we shall encounter in the next chapter). So overall, she bore a squashed appearance, as of clothing, hastily scrumpled. But in the middle of this rather odd face was a pair of large grey eyes, the colour of dirty dishwater but with a glow of love about them – though where Miss Baggage Jones could have acquired such a thing in her short, loveless existence was a puzzle. And yet it was this very quality – this love, shall we call it – that made her stop short at the sound of the baby's wails.

"Why? What 'ave we here?" she exclaimed. "Pots an' pans an' pat-a-cakes! A baby – in the snow!"

Baggage peered down at the angry red-faced infant, who instantly stopped crying and stared at her, dark button eyes wet with tears.

"Why, who d'you belong to?" said Baggage, looking around, trying to see where this miraculous infant might have sprung from – for, having no mother to educate her on such matters, she was still a little hazy on where babies actually came from. But, seeing nothing and no one to whom the babe might belong, she bent down to pick up the child.

"You poor little mite, you!" she declared. "Ain't got no one to love you, nor feed you – leavin' you out in the snow on this terrible night. 'Tis a shame, tha's what it is!"

The baby seemed to agree with her, for she was placated to be in Baggage's arms and even more contented when Baggage tore a strip of bread from the package she was carrying and gave it to the babe to suck on.

Baggage looked around again. Several good citizens of the parish passed by, turning their eyes hastily away as good taste dictated. Baggage knew why and she did not judge them. For her fourteen years had impressed upon her strongly that girls were baggage to be discarded.

But somehow she found it impossible to act upon this incontrovertible law of the land.

"Why, what am I to do wit' you?" asked Baggage, as if the baby might have an answer. "Can't leave you here – woutn't be right." Then she sighed heavily, her big dishwater eyes wide with alarm. "Only one thing for it, I s'pose!"

Chapter 3

In which we are introduced to the Black Jack Gaming
Hell of Camberwell Grove and the owner of the Spoon

"**O**ne thing for it", as it turned out, was Baggage bundling the infant under her threadbare cloak and smuggling her back to the only home she'd ever known.

A word is needed here about the Black Jack Gaming Hell where Baggage resided. A large house at the top of Camberwell Grove, located south of the Thames where the city of London straggled out and expired, the Black Jack was owned by the formidable Madam Manzoni-Jones (more of whom later). This place had earned a reputation as one of the blackest gaming hells in England. By which I mean, a place where extremely well-off young gentlemen – lords, baronets-to-be, heirs to dukedoms, even minor members of royalty –

came to throw away extremely large fortunes, playing hazard and faro and *rouge et noir* at the gaming tables. Peers of the realm and foolish young pigeons and venerable members of parliament had been known to lose reputations, fortunes – nay, entire inheritances – on a game of cards or a roll of the dice under the roof of the Black Jack.

Baggage worked in the kitchen, where she had been brought she knew not when nor why, at some time perhaps in the same hazy period of history when her name had been lost. Here she was employed under the strict auspices of the cook and housekeeper Mrs Spanks, a tall, hot poker of a woman whose motto was "Spare the spoon and spoil the child" (the spoon in question being that giant wooden implement with which Baggage came into regular contact).

Also resident at the Black Jack were Madam Manzoni herself, Mr Scapegrace – her lawyer and accountant – and half a dozen "Butterflies". These beautiful painted creatures fluttered through the gaming rooms where they dealt cards for extremely high stakes, poured whisky in extremely liberal measure and encouraged extremely foolhardy gentlemen into parting with more money at the tables than they could afford. Meanwhile the Butterflies learned to count cards, cheat at poker, pick pockets, and wheedle and cajole their favourites into hazarding fortunes for their favours. This they did until their bloom faded, at which point they were cast aside and new silky-winged creatures installed in their place.

Baggage's one great dream had been to be a Butterfly but at fourteen years her face remained a crumpled disappointment – more of a singed moth than a red admiral or a painted lady – so in the kitchen she stayed, under the auspices of the Spoon, and there she seemed destined to remain.

When Baggage returned that snowy night with the babe in arms, her first aim was to keep her from the view of the Spank and her Spoon. So she made her way straight to the Butterflies' boudoir – the salon where those winged creatures were getting ready for the evening trade. She burst in, damp and snow-covered, to find a dozen or so beautiful creatures lounging on velvet pouffes in tattered silk dressing gowns, lazily applying make-up in front of liver-spotted mirrors. They were a listless bunch, pale and sad-eyed beneath the paint, but when Baggage declared, "A baby – I found me a snow baby," they crowded round the little grub excitedly, lit up like Chinese lanterns.

"Where'd you find such a fing, Baggage?" demanded Birdy.

"You think Madam will let you keep her?" cooed Pearl-of-the-Night.

"Wha's her name?" This was Cleopatra (Cleo for short: all of the Butterflies had inherited their names from long-lost predecessors – handed down to each newcomer along with the tattered silk gowns and glittering paste jewels of her trade.)

"Her name is Twill," said Baggage, who had decided during the journey here that the little one deserved a proper name to call her own. "Cos when she stopped crying, she made the most lovely twilling noise – like a little bird."

At this point we must suppose Miss Baggage meant a trill, but having received only the scantiest of education, most of it via Mrs Spanks's Spoon, we should not judge her mistake too harshly.

"Twill Jones is her name," said Baggage, as proud as any new mother. "And Madam must let me keep her, else what'll become of her!"

The Butterflies were all in agreement but since all their lives were utterly at the mercy of Manzoni, and all were liable to be thrown out at her will, they privately had their doubts.

And at that moment, as if to embody those very doubts, Mrs Spanks appeared in the doorway to the boudoir, wielding the Spoon.

"What," she demanded, raising that culinary weapon aloft in a most alarming manner, "on 'eaven and earth is *that*?"

Chapter 4

*In which we meet the monstrous Madam Manzoni
and witness the swallowing of a human being in
her own flesh*

Baggage had been summoned to Madam Manzoni,
which could mean nothing good. This veritable
prodigy of a woman – iron lady of the Black Jack of
Camberwell Grove – was permanently installed in her
"morning room", where she resided in a chair-cum-
bed through morning, noon and night, unmoved and
unmoving for over half a century. Indeed, nobody alive
– save perhaps Mr Scapegrace, her resident lawyer –
could bear testimony to having seen her move from
there in living memory.

How had she become thus entrapped? The truth
was that Madam Manzoni had once been a diminutive
woman – with a tiny, bird-like frame – of singular
beauty. But over the years a monstrous accumulation

of flesh had descended upon her tiny body like lava upon a doomed city, burying the fairy-like girl in waves and waves of white undulating flesh. Her small face was still visible within a Saturn-like circle of chins and her tiny hands floated and fluttered over her giant form so that Baggage sometimes thought she could see the small girl of old trying to claw her way out of the giant, elderly woman's frame.

How Madam Manzoni had come to own the Black Jack was also shrouded in mystery. Some said she had once been mistress to the Prince Regent; others that she had made her money in the American gold mines of Missouri. Some audaciously suggested that she had once been a Butterfly herself, though to compare her to such will o' th' wisps seemed unthinkable. Whatever the case, Medora Manzoni-Jones now ruled the Black Jack with an iron fist, and though she was bodily confined to the morning room, her roaming gaze extended through every region of the house, thanks to the spying eyes of Mrs Spanks. And it was Spanks who had informed her mistress of the new arrival.

"So, Baggage!" Madam Manzoni surveyed the girl with tiny beady eyes that glimmered like currants in the swelling pudding of her doughy face. "You seem to grow more ugly by the day. Is this how you repay my kindness? Have I not provided you with a home all these years? I fondly imagined you might one day burst from your cocoon to join the Butterfly boudoir, and yet you have stubbornly insisted on becoming more hideous with each year that passes." She laughed – an oddly high-pitched sound that seemed out of place coming from her monstrous form.

"I – I – I'm sorry, Ma'am," stammered Baggage. "I have *tried* to get prettier..."

"You know the rules of the Black Jack, Baggage," oozed Madam Manzoni. "Beauty is your duty! Once a Butterfly loses her bloom, she's out – and even a kitchen maid in this establishment must at least attempt to be ornamental."

Baggage's already crumpled face dropped and her eyes pooled with muddy-looking tears. Life under the Spoon might be a bruising sort of existence but the Black Jack kitchens were the only home she had ever known. Fortunately, just at that moment, the Manzoni woman was distracted by the sight of what Baggage was holding.

"What," she demanded, "are those?"

"These, Madam?" Baggage sniffed loudly and held up a plate of miniature éclairs – a patisserie delicacy that she had been working on in the kitchen and was close to perfecting. Madam's tiny black eyes lit up and her little white hands fluttered in the direction of the plate.

Alas, Madam's bosom was now so colossal that it was impossible for her even to feed herself, so Baggage obligingly stepped forward and popped one of the mini delicacies in Madam's open bird-like mouth.

It had the desired effect.

For while Baggage might never earn a place in the Butterfly boudoir by her looks, her tenure at the Black Jack would surely always be assured by her baking. Mrs Spanks the cook was Madam's spymaster general, but her puddings were stodgy and her pies soggy-bottomed, and it was Baggage's cream puffs and choux buns, her peach turnovers and ganache horns that made Madam Manzoni's chins wobble with delight. And if Baggage knew her power to soften Madam's moods with her pastry wizardry, she also knew she had never needed it more than in this moment.

"It's a new recipe I've been working on," said Baggage. "Do you like it?"

"Not bad," said Madam Manzoni, licking her lips with a satisfied purr. "Quite satisfactory! Now, what's this I hear from Mrs Spanks about you bringing a baby into the house?"

"I found her, Madam, and I wondered…" Baggage took a deep breath. "Oh, won't you let me keep her?"

"*Her?*" Madam Manzoni's eyes lit up as they had for the cakes. "Bring the baby to me … and some more of those éclairs while you are at it."

Chapter 5

*In which Baggage makes a deal and
Twill finds a home*

T will, by the time Baggage brought her to Madam
Manzoni, was in a state of great contentment.
She had been fed on rich warm milk and washed and
cleaned and was now lying in a crate that had once
contained aged whisky, looking cherubic, with her
big blue eyes, dark curling lashes and a smattering of
golden curls upon her head.

"Well, well," said Madam, when the babe was lifted
so that she might see her better. "What a pretty little
caterpillar. Where did you say you found the creature,
Baggage?"

"In a rubbish heap," said Baggage. "She looked so
cold and hungry. I coutn't just leave 'er, ma'am!"

"You have a kind heart, Baggage," said Madam, her

20

chins trembling as she spoke. "But how exactly were you planning to feed her, pay for her keep – hmm?"

"I d-don't know, Ma'am," stammered Baggage. "I thought—"

"Did you, Baggage? Did you really *think*? A child is an expensive thing to rear. An investment. The outlay in food alone is considerable, and then there is clothing to think of, other expenses. Did you think of that?"

"No, Ma'am but I hoped—"

"Hoped?" Madam's chins now wobbled so violently that Baggage was reminded of a giant blancmange. "Hope won't put food on the table or money in the bank. You cannot raise a child on hope alone!"

"She can share my food," said Baggage – quite sincere in the offer, even though she herself subsisted on the meanest scraps from the kitchen leftovers and often went to bed hungry. "Oh, Madam, please!"

As it happened, Madam Manzoni had already made up her mind, but she waved her little white hand to indicate that Baggage should feed her another éclair. Then, with her mouth full of chocolate and cream, she heaved her colossal bosom and gave an expressive shrug.

"Very well, you may keep her. But on certain conditions."

"Oh, Madam, anything!"

"It will be your responsibility to keep her out of the way of the Black Jack clientele – no bother, not a whimper are we to hear. It must be as if she were invisible and inaudible."

"Oh yes, Madam," said Baggage, and Twill herself responded with a gurgle to express her delight and compliance.

"Caring for her must not interfere with your regular work," Madam went on, licking her lips to catch the last of the cream.

"It won't, Madam. I promise!"

"I will agree to feed and clothe the child but she will be indentured to me." Madam Manzoni paused and Baggage obligingly popped another éclair into her waiting lips so that her next words were delivered through a mouthful of pastry. "Mr Scapegrace will draw up a contract. As soon as she is old enough, she must repay the debt she has incurred."

"Yes, yes!" In truth, Baggage wasn't quite sure what an indenture was but she would have said anything to keep Twill.

"And if she blossoms." Madam Manzoni's eyes glittered as she eyed the little grub in the box. "If she grows pretty wings, then one day she may enter the

Butterfly boudoir."

Baggage's heart fluttered anxiously, but baby Twill cooed and beamed from her box as if in assent – and thus her fate was sealed.

Chapter 6

In which time passes and Twill grows wings

The passing of years wrought many changes across the land. A new young queen came to the throne; a group of downtrodden heroes rose up to fight for the vote – and lost; the first railway opened in London; the fashion for greatcoats came – and went; the iniquitous practice of slavery was abolished – throughout the British Empire at least; and a fire – reputedly started by a jealous mistress – destroyed Lloyd's Coffee House.

In the Black Jack Gaming Hell, change was also afoot. Baggage herself had grown older but no more beautiful, saved from the rubbish heap only by ever more extraordinary feats of patisserie magic. She had taken to asking Bob, the errand boy from the local butcher's shop, to search out the latest exotic ingredients – herbs and spices and suchlike – on his trips to Borough Market. These she whisked, folded and wove into ever more glorious culinary concoctions. Since Bob did not share the general view on Baggage's appearance (having a fondness for dishwater-grey eyes and finding her crumpled face reminded him of the lopsided buns to which he was very partial) he was always happy to oblige, and thus Baggage's baking kept her firmly in Madam Manzoni's employ.

Time, as our good readers probably know, had made a great impression on the life of the young man known as Oliver Twist. He had passed from orphan-who-asked-for-more; to the runaway undertaker's apprentice; to pickpocket-vagabond and smallest member of a gang of housebreakers; to the cherished and adored adopted heir to Mr Brownlow. His fortunes had dipped and roller-coastered and finally risen, and he now sat enthroned in his guardian's heart as the most beloved and fortunate of boys.

And time had wrought great changes upon his sister too. Young Twill was now – at nearly thirteen years of age – clearly no longer a grub by anyone's standards. Brought up in the Black Jack kitchens but protected from the Spoon by Baggage (who had proved herself as fierce as Mrs Spanks in defence of her darling),

Twill had grown into a girl of warm heart, peerless beauty and dauntless temper. For whereas her twin brother Oliver had grown up unloved and neglected for the first decade of his life, Twill was the darling of the Black Jack. Everyone adored her – everyone except Mrs Spanks. The Butterflies petted her, Baggage doted on her, and she was the apple in the rheumy eye of Mr Scapegrace, the wiry old lawyer who stayed at the Black Jack who-knew-why. In any case, Twill was a universal favourite.

The Butterflies taught Twill the art of card-playing and face-painting; Baggage imparted the wisdom of buttercream and blind baking; and Mr Scapegrace taught her to read and write – for Baggage insisted that her Twill should be raised to greater things than the boudoir. In fact, she had long since come to the realisation that life as a Butterfly was as short-lived and precarious as it was glamorous, and she wanted better for Twill.

She was thus determined that her darling should be educated and it had not been difficult to persuade Mr Scapegrace to take on the task of "reading and writing her", as Baggage put it. The little mole of a man, who spent his days behind a desk, buried under piles of promissory notes and pawnbrokers' slips and deeds of title, refused to accept the pennies Baggage offered him in return for this education. For Twill proved a most delightful pupil – quick, eager to learn and with an insatiable curiosity – so that poor dear, dusty Mr Scapegrace soon found the hour he spent with the girl to be the highlight of his day.

And what of Twill herself – of her hopes and dreams? Well, when she wasn't skivvying in the Black Jack kitchens, or reading tales of Arabian nights and Trojan horses or puzzling through the riddles of Pythagoras with Mr Scapegrace, Twill lived the life of intrepid adventurer and explorer to rival the great Dr Livingstone himself – and the borough of Southwark was her kingdom.

Twill Jones of the Black Jack was considered the out-and-out leader of the Camberwell Grove kids – the collection of scraps and urchins, kitchen girls and errand boys from Grove Lane right the way up to Denmark Hill. She devised their games, egged them to feats of daring, and organised their raids and battles against the railway workers' kids from Peckham Rye.

She liked to read in Mr Scapegrace's books of lands far away, of epic battles fought, pirates on the high seas, of mangrove swamps and rainforests swarming with monkeys and birds of every colour – and she dreamed one day of going to all those places. For now the scope of her existence stretched only from Forest Hill to Dulwich Village, but her imagination populated those streets and parks and alleyways with elephants and lions, bloodthirsty plunderers, swamps, forests, coral reefs and golden sands where buried treasures lay.

And so Twill grew up, happy as a sparrow, content as one of the stray cats that lived off scraps from the Black Jack kitchens. The only regrettable consequence of the passing years, as Baggage saw it, was that Twill had begun to show signs of turning into the most glorious of Butterflies. And Baggage was not wrong. If her brother had been considered a cherubic-looking child, Twill shared all his angelic beauty, but her big blue eyes also shone with a fierce light and there was a determined tilt to her chin and firm set to her rose-petal mouth that reflected her fearless temper.

And now Baggage's every effort was invested in keeping this information from Madam Manzoni. The Butterflies were all enlisted in the effort. Where once they had enjoyed painting the little girl with rouge and wrapping her in their finest silks, now she was banned from the boudoir, allowed to wear only the meanest of rags and, of late, Baggage had resorted to covering her darling's face with soot to prevent Mrs Spanks from catching a glimpse of the beauty of which Twill herself was unaware.

"Why must I have muck all over my face?" Twill demanded one cold March morning as Baggage dabbed her nose with coal dust from the fireplace and bundled her golden curls roughly up under a grubby mob-cap, which she insisted Twill wear at all times. "I mean, I don't mind. It's handy when we're trying to ambush the Peckham Rye posse, but—"

"I told you," said Baggage. "It protects you from…"

"From what, Baggage?" Twill gazed at her beloved Baggage – whom she regarded as part mother, part older sister – with a curious smile.

"From bad things," Baggage said hastily, with a tilt of her chin and a twist of her lips that forbade Twill to ask any more. "Now, enough wi' your questions, missy! There's fires to be laid an' a million an' one jobs besides. Today is a big day in the Black Jack an' I don't have time for your endless questions. Save those for Mr Scapegrace an' your book learnin'!"

It was indeed a big day and all the inhabitants of the Black Jack were in a flutter of excitement. Madam Manzoni had recently had word that one of her most regular young pigeons, the son of the Duke of Whatshisname-or-Whatever (nobody was quite sure what or where) had that day come into his inheritance. This was in consequence of the unfortunate death of his father, who had choked on a ruby signet ring. His son – now the new young Duke of Whatshisname-or-Wherever – was known for his wild and reckless ways and his gloriously bad luck at cards. He was one of the best contributors to the Black Jack roll of debtors and Madam Manzoni had great hopes that, now that he was a man of means, he might finally be able to discharge his outstanding bill – and then contrive to lose the rest of his newly acquired fortune at her tables.

To this end, a great party was being thrown in the young Duke of Whatshisname's honour. No expense was to be spared to christen the new peer of the realm, and so everyone in the Black Jack was in a flat spin, polishing the plates, bringing up the best champagne from the cellars, preparing lobster tureen, turtle soup, pigeon pie and all the other little delicacies that the new Duke of Whatshisname was known to favour.

The centrepiece of the celebratory feast was to be a giant confectionary creation – a coming-of-age cake to be presented to Madam's new favourite client. Baggage had been ordered to bring this patisserie production to life in just a few short hours, and when Madam

Manzoni called for her morning cup of chocolate and petit-fours, Baggage was in the middle of a particularly tricky feat of spun sugar work that demanded no interruption.

"Let the girl take it," said Mrs Spanks, nodding over to where Twill was polishing a pile of silver spoons.

"No!" Baggage looked up from her sugar artistry in alarm. "But – she … can't!"

"Oh – and why *can't* she?" said Mrs Spanks, wielding her Spoon in a most interesting manner.

"I can go!" Baggage declared. But as she was currently at a critical moment in the process of creating a sugary-light birds' nest to replicate the pigeon on the new duke's coat of arms, this statement was evidently insupportable.

"Madam asked for *the girl!*" said Mrs Spanks, with a triumphant glimmer in her eye. For, in truth, Mrs Spanks had for some time been aware of both Twill's burgeoning beauty and Baggage's attempts to hide it from Madam Manzoni. She had kept this knowledge to herself, biding her time and holding her patience, waiting for the most opportune moment to share it with her employer.

And now that moment had come.

"She … she asked for her?" Baggage's arms dropped

and the sugar nest teetered precariously.

"Most particularly. Wants to discuss her indenture, I'm told…" Mrs Spanks spun the Spoon like a baton and Baggage's eyes widened in alarm, putting the nest in yet more jeopardy.

"I'll go!" said Twill after Spanks had left, unaware of the jeopardy she was in. "I'll be in and out in no time."

"Here." Baggage kept one hand on the endangered sugar work, and with the other scooped a mess of chocolate ganache from the pot at her side and smeared it on Baggage's face. Then she contorted her whole body to grab some cinders from the fires and apply them to Twill's face, all the while continuing to feather the Duke's nest with sugary additions.

"What you doing to me, Baggage?" Twill protested, blinking her eyes and coughing as the coal dust caught in her throat.

"Never should 'ave allowed 'er to grow so beautiful…" Baggage was muttering to herself. "Foolish, foolish… Now, can you squint your eye a little – so?"

Twill attempted a squint which seemed to only half satisfy Baggage.

"When she addresses you, I want you to talk out of the corner of your mouth – as if half your face was frozen," Baggage went on, doing such a comical impression that it made Twill giggle.

"This is no laughin' matter!" Baggage insisted, continuing to spin the sugar. "You an' I both knows that a Butterfly's career is over in the flutter of a wing. You're too good for that, my Twill." She looked so desperately sad that Twill stopped giggling. "P'rhaps stoop a little." Baggage continued to think. "Or maybe if I popped in a little somethin' to give you an 'ump…"

Baggage was looking around for a dishcloth to stuff down the back of Twill's blouse, and wondering if a bit of dough might serve to create a malformed nose, when Mrs Spanks reappeared, looking ready to do battle with the Spoon as her sabre.

"Hurry up, girl! Madam is calling for her sweetmeats! She particularly asked for violet creams!"

"I promise I'll be in and out in a moment," said Twill to the anxious-looking Baggage. "She'll barely notice me!"

"Lawks, girl!" said Baggage, surveying her hasty handiwork with anxiety. "You best hope she don't, or we is all in a world of trouble!"

Chapter 7

In which the dangers of beauty are expounded and
Baggage makes a big decision

T will was incorrect in thinking she would pass
unnoticed. Madam Manzoni prided herself on
knowing everything that happened within the walls
of the Black Jack. Though she never strayed from her
chaise-longue she knew every detail of what passed
under her roof, largely thanks to the good offices of
Mrs Spanks and Mr Scapegrace. And, in truth, she had
been wondering of late about the little girl Baggage
had found in the snow. Mr Scapegrace, normally her
most attentive and obliging of household spies, was
decidedly unforthcoming about the girl, describing her
as "barely noteworthy … slow, dull … disappointing,"
and Mrs Spanks – her less adoring but no less willing
informant – had also been rather lacking with

information. Until this morning.

Mrs Spanks had a taste for drama and had thus awaited the optimum moment to impart the news of Twill's budding beauty to her mistress. Baggage's baking had raised her in the old lady's esteem to an extent that Mrs Spanks had come to resent, and on this day when the coming-of-age cake look set to crown Baggage's triumph, Mrs Spanks had seen her chance to bring her rival down.

And so it was that, while Mr Scapegrace had described the girl as unremarkable, Mrs Spanks now imparted quite another tale. Indeed, her eyes glimmered with such delicious malice as she spoke of the little girl's charms that Madam had grown quite impatient to see her. And the revelation could not have been more timely.

For some time now, the latest Pearl-of-the-Night had been looking a little ragged-around-the-edges. She was nearing the grand old age of twenty-five, and Madam Manzoni was thinking it was time to let this Butterfly loose in the garden. She would be needing a new Pearl to grace the piquet table, and tonight was a perfect opportunity to inaugurate Baggage's girl into the Butterfly boudoir.

Twill was unaware of any of this as she entered the

room, back hunched, eye scrunched, mouth lopsided. She had added in a little drooling and a dragging leg for good measure, basing her performance on that of the old signalman up at Denmark Hill station who walked with a lolloping stomp. Nonetheless, she took no chances, approaching Madam Manzoni from behind her chaise-longue, hoping to place her tray of violet creams on the little table without being seen at all. And if it hadn't been for the books she might have got away with it.

It was the books that were the problem. Twill had never been in Madam's morning room before, and nobody had told her that there were shelves lined with volume upon volume (though Madam had never opened a single one – and there was some suspicion that they weren't real books at all, but only a decorative collection of leather spines). And therein lay the problem. For the collection in Mr Scapegrace's dusty little office was modest, and Twill had read most of its contents at least three times and had lately begun to long for more variety in her literary diet. And now here she was confronted with a leather-bound feast.

"Is that you, Baggage?" demanded Madam, who had been alerted by the odd drag of Twill's foot. She strained to turn her mountainous form without success.

"No, Ma'am – it'sh Twill," she attempted to lisp.

"Ah, Baggage's girl! Excellent! Excellent! Let me see you – come into the light."

Alas, as Twill stepped forward she was so taken by the sight of a slim volume by Mr Walter Scott that she had been particularly longing to read that she momentarily forgot her hunchbacked, drooling persona and stood for a moment in a shaft of sunlight from the big bay windows, transfixed by the sight. And she wore a look of such bright wonder that even the ganache and cinders could not obscure the beauty beneath.

And that is how Madam Manzoni-Jones beheld Twill for the second time in her life.

"Well, well!" declared Madam, her own eyes sparkling like two small gems. "The little snow baby has grown into quite a beauty."

"Oh – um – indeed no, ma'am," said Twill coming to herself and remembering what Baggage had told her about not being beautiful at any cost. "Indeed I am very, very ugly." She quickly attempted to rearrange her face as Baggage had instructed, hoiking up her shoulder in her best impression of a hump, but her efforts were too late for the old matriarch, who, accustomed to the Butterflies' attempts to paint over their faded looks, was just as quick to see through Twill's charade.

"Come a little closer, snow girl!" she said, waggling a tiny white finger, an expression on her face that Twill was powerless to disobey. As she stepped forward, the claw-like hand shot out, grabbing her wrist, wrenching Twill so that her face was just inches from the old woman's.

"Fancy that," said Madam, eyes alert and glistening. "A regular pearl in the pigswill. You remind me of myself when I was your age."

Twill's eyes widened with alarm and astonishment.

The old woman laughed, a tinkling high-pitched sound. "I do declare, you are just the thing – the very thing, my dear!"

"For – um – what, Madam?" said Twill, forgetting her lisp in her alarm.

"The icing on the cake, the cherry on the tree – the shining star in tonight's sky. Who more fitting than a brand-new Butterfly to present the coming-of-age cake? A new duke and a new Butterfly!"

"What – me? In the Black Jack?" stammered Twill, caught momentarily between excitement at the idea of a new adventure (a lifetime of being strictly shut out of the gaming rooms had only heightened her curiosity to glimpse what went on within!) and horror at what Baggage would say.

"Certainly, my dear. Tonight, you will be my latest Butterfly. A new Pearl, perhaps?"

Twill gasped in horror. She, like everyone in the Black Jack, was only too aware of the perilous position of the current Pearl-of-the-Night. Indeed, it had been the main topic of conversation in the Butterfly boudoir for some months now. Baggage had been preparing all sorts of face poultices; and Bob the butcher's boy had procured a detoxing concoction from a Moorish gypsy in Dulwich Village; even Mr Scapegrace had been reading up on ancient rejuvenating practices such as sleeping with a rabbit's foot and drinking backwards and standing on your head for ten minutes a day – all of which were designed to keep poor Pearl's skin young, her forehead wrinkle free and her hair clear of the telltale silver threads that would surely lead to her ejection from the Black Jack.

"But ... you already have a Pearl!" said Twill.

"Yes, and I suppose the girl has not quite outlived her usefulness – yet!" Madam Manzoni mused, before waving her hand decisively. "Indeed, now I think on it, my dear, I believe a new name is required. Nothing recycled." Madam managed to raise an eyebrow, like a slug wriggling on a vast mountain of lard. "Yes, you need – a *nom de papillon* all of your own. Brighter than a

pearl – hmm – a crystal, perhaps? No, a gem, a jewel…
You, my dear, are that rarest of gems. A diamond!"

"A … diamond?" asked Twill.

"Yes, a diamond! You shall be my Snow Diamond,"
declared Madam Manzoni with a glitter of triumph.
"And tonight, my dear, will be your chance to dazzle!"

Chapter 8

*In which Bob proves to be a young man of substance
and a flight plan for the newest Butterfly is hatched*

While all this was going on, Baggage had
completed the sugar nest and – to her great
consternation – had been sent out on an "emergency
errand". More sugared almonds were required for
Duke Whatshisname's coming-of-age cake and none
were to be had closer than Lordship Lane. Mrs Spanks
had insisted that Baggage procure them herself – none
other could be spared she said, with a gleam of malice
in her eyes, even when Baggage protested that the
ganache filling could not afford to wait, let alone
the chocolate mirror glaze. So to Lordship Lane
Baggage hurried, her heart a-quiver and her head in
a spin, thinking of Twill and Manzoni – and by the
time she returned to the Black Jack kitchens she was

confronted with a most unnerving sight.

For there was Twill, bathed, scented, painted, primped and dressed in a gown that Madam Manzoni had sent down from her own wardrobe – a white sugary confection with puffed sleeves, mountains of underskirts like layers of a wedding cake and sewn with tiny glass gems and diamonds made of paste that made it glitter like a snowflake. Her hair – at Madam Manzoni's direction – had been elaborately curled, a dab of rouge applied to her cheeks and lips, and a drop of perfume applied behind ears that had been hung with tiny paste diamonds on strings. The whole effect was simply...

"Horrible! Horrible!" wailed Baggage when she set eyes upon her snow baby, now transformed into an ice princess. "What has she done to you?"

"Madam wants her to present the cake to the new duke in the gaming parlour tonight," said Cleo, who had been fixing the little earrings to Twill's lobes with a thread.

"They are calling her the Snow Diamond!" said Birdy.

"Medora hasn't christened a new Butterfly since the king's father was on the throne!" declared Mr Scapegrace, who had made a rare venture from his study to witness Twill's transformation. He had a wistful expression on his papery old face as he beheld her, while the collection of Butterflies giggled, most of them having never heard Madam Manzoni referred to by her first name – or even really imagined that she had one!

"No, no, no!" said Baggage, her crumpled face glowing with anger. "I won't have my Twill in among the gambling and the drinking and the swearing and who knows what else, till she grows old and is thrown out on the flower heap! I won't have it."

"But what's the alternative?" mumbled Mr Scapegrace, peering through his glasses like a mole. "Where else can the girl go? Medora will never allow her to stay on any other terms."

"I know where she can go!"

Everyone turned to see who had made this pronouncement. And there stood Bob the butcher's boy, holding a brace of pheasants and looking extremely pleased with himself.

A word here about Bob the butcher's boy. He was, despite his name, no longer a boy – indeed he had not been boyish for over a decade. But he was small of stature and had the soft, plump features of a newborn and not much more hair on his head than a babe-in-arms either. This made it hard to tell if he were eleven or one hundred and eleven, and thus he had been addressed as "boy" since he was the former and probably would remain so until he was the latter.

He had also been in love with Baggage since he was old enough to remember, and probably would be till he was old enough not to, and he might easily continue to that grand old age without ever plucking up the courage to tell her. Baggage herself was mighty fond of Bob, but since it never occurred to her that anyone could fall in love with her, she never noticed that he had.

Bob showed his devotion by procuring for Baggage little delicacies and spices that she might experiment with in her baking, while she in turn saved him morsels of her latest sweetmeats to sample, and both were pretty well satisfied with the arrangement, save Bob did dream sometimes of planting a kiss on Baggage's sweet pudding of a face and calling her his currant bun.

That same face turned to him now, alight with love, anger and despair, and Bob thought she had never looked so beautiful. In fact, it was all he could do not to clasp her in his arms and ask her to be his apple turnover! Instead he pulled himself up to his tallest height – nearly achieving five foot in the process –

pushed back his shoulders and declared, "They be wanting a kitchen maid. In a house I deliver to over in Clerkenwell way. Twill's the right age. She might go there!"

For a second he wondered if he had said the wrong thing, as silence reigned in the Black Jack kitchens. But then Baggage's eyes lit up and she grabbed his face in both hands and planted a kiss on his astonished lips.

"That's perfect! The very thing! Do you think they'd take her?"

Still reeling from the kiss, which had tasted of sugared almonds and newly baked bread rolls – and something that he imagined was the very taste of heaven itself – Bob stammered, "Why – um – that is … I don't see why not!"

"It would offer an alternative for the child," Mr Scapegrace was saying, peering through his spectacles as if weighing up the situation like a contract.

"Though she do look so beautiful!" murmured Pearl-of-the-Night, gazing wistfully at the vision in white.

"Well, she can be beautiful north of the river!" declared Baggage. "There's no time to lose if we want her out before the mistress gets wind of our plan."

"You're … sending me away?"

Everyone turned to Twill, who was as pale as a

snowflake in her Butterfly garb. Baggage took a step towards her darling and looked at her with an expression of such love it made her dishwater eyes glow. "You know I'd keep you by me side till me dyin' day, but I always knew this day would come, though it breaks me 'eart to see it come around so soon."

"But – but – this is my home…" said Twill. She'd had a most extraordinary morning. After the initial horror of discovery, she had rather enjoyed her transformation into the Snow Diamond and had even started to look forward to catching a glimpse of life behind the doors of the gaming parlours, meeting the strange species she had heard the Butterflies talk of – profligate young gentlemen known as "Greeks", the silly dupes they called "Pigeons" and the scoundrels known as "Captain Sharps". She'd been excited about presenting Lord Whatshisname with his cake and being lauded as the newest and brightest of the Black Jack Butterflies. Now she was being told she was to be sent away – away from the only home she had ever known, the only family.

"The Butterflies are my sisters, Mr Scapegrace is like an uncle and you, Baggage … you're my…" She wanted to say that Baggage was like a mother to her, but the words stopped on lips that were glossed cherry pink and trembling. "You're my Baggage!" was all that came out.

"And I will always be your Baggage," declared that good lady. "But I ditn't save you from the rubbish 'eap only for Madam to throw you right back there. So there's no time to waste."

Chapter 9

*In which Twill departs the Black Jack and takes her
destiny with her, wrapped in a twist of paper*

In barely half an hour's time, Twill was back in her
old clothes, her hair neatly piled back into a modest
cap, a clean apron round her tidy little waist and a new
pair of stockings on her feet. She had a small bundle
packed with some morsels of food for the journey,
a spare apron and cap, and a pocket handkerchief
embroidered with her initials.

Bob the butcher's boy had errands in Clerkenwell
and could take Twill to the house he had mentioned
that very afternoon. Farewells were hasty before Mrs
Spanks or Madam Manzoni could learn of her flight,
and poor Baggage – who had been like a whirlwind
in readying her girl for departure – suddenly found
herself pushing back tears as Twill stood before her,

good to go. She had said her goodbyes to the Butterflies and even to Mr Scapegrace – who had pressed a copy of the latest novel by Mr Scott into her hands and told her not to abandon her Greek – but faced with her beloved Baggage, Twill wasn't sure she could hold it all together.

"If you love your old Baggage, you'll promise me summat?" said that good lady, who was trying to look extremely fierce in an effort not to cry.

"Anything, anything."

"Promise you will leave 'ere an' never come back," said Baggage. "No matter wha' happens!"

"Never?" Twill stared in astonishment and horror. "But then … I'll – never see you again."

"That's as may be," said Baggage, though in truth the prospect near on broke her dear warm oven of a heart. "But I need you to promise."

Poor Twill gazed at her Baggage, who had saved her that snowy night, given her more than a mother's love, raised her with such care and never asked anything in return. How could she refuse her this one last request? Yet how could she grant it?

"I – I promise," said Twill, the words tearing a hole in her heart as she uttered them.

"Good girl!" Baggage sniffed loudly and nodded

her head violently to ward off the flood of dishwater pooling in her eyes. "An' take this." She handed Twill a little kid bag, containing a tiny twist of paper wrapped around something small and round – the size of a penny, perhaps.

"What is it?"

"I found it on you – that night in the snow – 'twas in the blanket you'd been left in, so truly it's yours and I was selfish to keep it from you till now," said Baggage. "I always thought of myself as your mother, see!"

"And so you are to me!" declared Twill. "I have never wanted any other!"

Baggage gave a sound somewhere between a sob and a hiccup, then pulled herself together and went on. "Maybe one day if you do…"

"I never will!" insisted Twill.

Baggage's whole frame shuddered at this pronouncement and it was with supreme difficulty that she uttered the rest. "Well, you 'ave this if that time should come. Keep it safe an' keep yourself safe too," she said. "Make your Baggage proud."

"I'll try," said Twill, with a crack in her voice that was most unlike the fierce leader of the Camberwell Grovers, for Twill Jones – who had long dreamed of adventuring far beyond the familiar streets and alleys of her home – now wanted nothing more than to be told she could stay at the Black Jack till her dying day.

"Go to your wide future," Baggage managed to declare. And then she wrapped Twill in a tight embrace from which she thought she might never be able to tear herself. When she eventually managed to do so, she scrunched up her crumpled dear old face and blinked away the tears: "Now, be off with you, me girl!"

And then Bob the butcher's boy was lifting Twill up beside him on the cart and giving Baggage a nod to say he'd look after her girl. And then the cart was off and away, down the lane of tall larch trees lining Camberwell Grove, into the city.

Chapter 10

In which Twill encounters a familiar face, though
she don't rightly recognise it at the time

Bob the butcher's boy had promised Baggage that her girl would be just fine, and it so happened that he was both right and wrong, about that and other matters.

As he drove along at a steady pace, with the dazed and heartbroken girl by his side, she might have shed a tear or two as they made their way along the long cart track towards the city, but Bob was enough of a gentleman that he pretended not to notice. And in truth her weeping soon dried up as they passed the Elephant and Castle and approached Waterloo Bridge, and Twill started to notice all the activity on the road into the city. She had never been into London before and the sights and sounds along the roadway thrilled the girl so much that she forgot about Baggage and the Butterflies.

Such an array of traffic was there on the road that day – flower sellers and fruit stalls, a man with a monkey, an organ grinder, a troop of May Day dancers, and a rag-and-bone man shouting out for "any old iron". The sun was shining as they approached the bridge and the light danced on the river and over all the little boats bobbing up and down in a way that made Twill think of pirates and perilous journeys to foreign lands and Robinson Crusoe on his island. And with such pleasant imaginings in her head it was difficult to remain completely unhappy.

They stopped at a coaching house, where Bob had errands to run. Twill climbed down off the cart and perched herself on a barrel in the mews where she watched the ostlers who ran to greet the great men's carriages and unharness their tired teams, racing to provide them with new horses for the next leg of their journey. All this was done with such speed and dexterity that Twill marvelled as she watched. Sometimes the owners of the carriages stayed in their equipages, ordering coffee and ale and mutton and bread to be brought to them from within the inn. Others stepped into the coaching house for a small meal before emerging contented to continue the next leg of the journey.

Bob was gone some time and so Twill entertained herself by watching the rich folk, trying to predict who would alight and who would remain in their carriages. A lady in a plumed hat and a gentleman in a greatcoat with so many capes it might have clothed a whole family of Peckham railway children chose to alight; but a pair of elderly ladies in powdered wigs and fur mufflers sat stiffly in their carriage, pooh-poohing the time it took to fix the horses.

At length an elderly gentleman with a young boy – his grandson, Twill guessed – arrived at the inn. The old man looked so frail, and the boy so solicitous for the old man's comfort, that Twill bet herself that they would alight. And indeed they did. She watched them from her barrel perch by the servants' entrance, and as the boy passed he caught her eye, and there was something so familiar in his glance, something so much like home in the expression of his eye, that Twill was sure she must know him, and yet at the same time she knew she had never seen him before.

The boy started as if she were known to him too. He was the same age as her, though he was slighter of build; he shared her flaxen hair and cornflower-blue eyes, though his had a milkier hue. And he was dressed in a smart sailor suit and well-shined shoes that must have cost ten times what her modest garb was worth. He looked, thought Twill, well cared for, and well loved, and for some reason this gave the girl a burst of pleasure she could scarce account for. Yet he neither seemed puffed up by good fortune, nor did he look down upon her, as some young gentlemen of his standing might. Instead he smiled, and she could not help but smile in return.

Yes, reader, you are quicker off the mark than our young heroine, for you must have guessed that Twill beheld none other than Oliver Twist, her long-lost twin brother – now grown into Master Twist-Brownlow, heir to the Brownlow fortune, and travelling off on an errand of some importance to his well-being and that of his guardian. But if there was a momentary flicker of recognition from either Twill or Twist it was over in an instant, as Mr Brownlow reached for Oliver's hand to steady his faltering gait, and Oliver engaged him in conversation about mutton or pudding for lunch. Then, with one last curious glance at the girl sitting on the barrel by the horse trough, he turned and was gone.

Chapter 11

In which another old friend is encountered, in
less than ideal circumstances

Two hours later, Twill found herself standing outside the house on Doughty Street where Bob had said they were advertising for a housemaid. Bob had business in Gray's Inn Road nearby but had said he would come and enquire after her when he was done. So now Twill found herself knocking on the scullery door, which was opened by a plump kitchen maid who eyed her suspiciously.

"Please, ma'am. I've come about the post."

The young woman – who might have been fifteen or sixteen years of age – was red-cheeked and large-bosomed, and had the appearance of a well-risen but rather lumpy loaf of bread.

"You got references, 'ave ya?"

"No, but I have been working in the kitchen of a large house in Camberwell since – well, since I was ever so small. I'm proper handy, Baggage says."

"Who's Baggage?" the loaf-of-bread girl demanded. "Your mistress?"

"No – she's ... my family. But Mrs Spanks said I wasn't completely useless. She was the cook – and housekeeper too."

The warm-loaf girl looked unconvinced. "She write you a reference, did she?"

"No ... I don't have any references, but—"

"No references, no interview. Tha's what the master says. Says 'is young mistress is in a delicate condition. Don't need to be troubled with no chancers with shady backgrounds knocking on the door, claimin' to 'ave experience – run away from their old posts cos they're workshy, more like." As she spoke, Twill got the impression that this girl was perhaps the *second* kitchen maid, previously bottom of the servant pile, but due to rise in the ranks with the arrival of a new underling, and enjoying her first exercise of power over an inferior.

"I'm a good worker," she insisted. "Strong and quick to learn and willing to do anything."

"No references – no chance!" said the girl.

"But if I might just speak with the housekeeper – or

the lady of the house!"

"Lady of the 'ouse don't have time for the likes of you. Be off with ya!" And with that, the girl slammed the door and Twill found herself suddenly jobless, homeless and hopeless, in an unfamiliar area of the great and bustling metropolis – and with no idea what to do next.

Clutching her bundle, she climbed the area steps and surveyed the street on which the house was located with an air of the unreal. City life was unfolding as normal even as hers seemed to have come to a premature end. Grand folks paraded in top hats and tails; a nanny pushed a baby in a giant perambulator; a shoeshine boy sat on a box by the corner, whistling for trade; a couple of ragamuffin children played with a hoop and stick; a flower seller sang an old ditty about a long-lost love.

What was she to do now? Baggage had made Twill promise never to return, but she had nowhere else to go. And she was really rather hungry – and any longings for adventure that she might have harboured earlier in this long and most peculiar day had now completely left her.

As it happened, at that very moment, the main door to the household opened, and from therein emerged the master of the house and his young mistress. She was a beautiful young creature, dark-haired and blue-eyed, much younger than her husband and with a brightness about her eye and a spot of pink in her cheek that had captured his heart. Twill caught sight of her and her heart leapt.

"M'lady!" she called.

The master and his young mistress were already down the steps and crossing the square, too caught up in one another to be aware of their surroundings. The young mistress's arm rested in the crook of her husband's elbow; her reticule hanging gaily from her other. She laughed at something her husband had said. Twill was nearly upon them now.

"Please, mistress – I beg your pardon, ma'am…"

And then it happened.

A boy – a shadow, he seemed, for he was so quick – darted between Twill and the woman. He wore a battered top hat, a scarlet waistcoat under a set of tails that had definitely seen better days, and broken hob-nailed boots that seemed somehow to move noiselessly across the cobbles. Twill saw his hand shoot out, grab the young lady's reticule and pop it into his pocket before departing so swiftly down an alley she half wondered if she had imagined it.

Twill felt several emotions at once. The first was an instantaneous instinct to give chase. Had she not been brought up hunting down the ragamuffins of Peckham Rye? She could run this top-hat boy down in minutes! The second feeling was an instinct to warn the young lady – to help her reclaim her possessions. Not just out of a sense of right and wrong that Baggage had instilled in her, but also from a third emotion: hope. Might there not be a reward for retrieving the young lady's possessions? Might she not look kindly on Twill's application for the post of kitchen maid?

"M'lady," she cried – tugging on the young lady's arm to attract her attention. "Your purse!"

Then she set off in pursuit of the top-hatted pocket-picker, shouting, "Stop, thief!"

And therein lay her downfall.

Chapter 12

*In which Twill becomes the victim of
mistaken identity*

It was somewhat unfortunate that what the young
lady turned to see was a rather poor-looking girl
(for though Baggage had done her best, Twill's attire
was of the meanest variety), and then the absence of
her purse – and then the girl fleeing. She put all this
together and reached quite the wrong conclusion.

"My purse – that girl stole my purse!" she cried,
breathless and bright-eyed, pointing to Twill's departing
figure.

"Stop, thief!" cried her husband, keen to be the
knight in shining armour for his young bride.

The shoeshine boy took up the cry, and so did the
boys playing hoop and ball. "Stop, thief!" they yelled.
The flower seller added a harmony: "Stop, thief!" And

this alerted a policeman who was doing his round on the corner and who set up the chase, hollering, "Stop, in the name of the law!" The husband too was on Twill's tail, to prove he was not too old for heroics, and so was the shoeshine boy – his eye upon a reward – and the hoop-and-ball kids joined in for the larks. And so, as the top-hatted urchin ran pell-mell down alleyways and byways, twisting and turning, ducking and diving, and Twill gave chase, behind her there came a veritable mob of pursuers, all chiming in with the cry: "Stop, thief!" and "Catch that girl!"

The top-hat thief ran up Mount Pleasant – that most ill-named district of the metropolis, where all the rubbish and detritus of London was dumped – past the Middlesex Prison, where petty criminals walked the treadmill in silence to atone for their crimes; past the Cold Baths, where the idle rich went to treat their rheumatism and gout. He ducked, he dived and he was fast; faster than any of the Camberwell Grovers, or the wiry-limbed Peckham railway children. But as she neared the corner by Farringdon Lane, Twill was sure she was gaining on the top-hat boy.

He turned into Pear Tree Court, Twill hot on his tail, both of them jostling past the drinkers outside the Crown Tavern then into the oasis on the periphery of the slums that was Clerkenwell Green, a place filled with booksellers and men giving out pamphlets and the buzz of ideas and words. Here Twill saw her chance. There was a cattle trough up ahead where a farmer had stopped to give his horse a drink. Twill recalled an ambush she had lately planned on the Peckham Rye kids and, quick as a flash, she vaulted over the cattle trough, cut off the top-hatted thief who had gone round it, and whipped the reticule out of his hand with a yell of triumph.

For a second the top-hatted thief stared at her in surprise, and Twill felt a momentary glow of triumph. Then she glanced behind and so did the top-hatted thief, and only then did she realise that the crowd was chasing her – and that she was now in possession of stolen goods!

"Stop, thief!" yelled the policeman.

"Stop that girl!" called the shoeshine boy.

And suddenly there was no sign of the top-hatted thief. He had vanished into thin air – and with him the proof of her innocence.

Once again Twill took to her heels – and she ran now not in pursuit but because she was being pursued. She was fast and resourceful, but the streets near Clerkenwell Green market were crowded, and trying to duck around the stalls selling fish and flowers and books and all manner of other paraphernalia was difficult. She didn't know this area as she did the alleys and lanes of Camberwell and Denmark Hill and Peckham Rye and so she was running blind – no object in view other than getting away now, all chance of gaining reward quite gone. She just needed to escape the angry claws of unfair justice that were closing in on her. What would happen if she were caught? Would she be put in jail? Or in the stocks? Or made to walk the treadmill? Or would she be a "lagger" – sent to Botany Bay for her crimes? She'd heard of children transported for the theft of a loaf of bread, and though she had longed for a trip to foreign climes this wasn't quite how she'd envisaged it.

She was heading deep into the city's most desperate slums now, and more and more people had joined the chase, enjoying the entertainment as they might a cockfight or a bout of bare-knuckle boxing. The streets around Hatton Garden were littered with detritus and stank of starvation – half-naked children crouching in doorways, rats and dogs and dead cats and streams of sewage running down the centre of each dingy thoroughfare. She rounded into an alley called Sixpence Lane. Her heart was beating so fast she felt as if it might burst out of her chest as she sprinted into Lilley Lane, where the dilapidated houses closed in on her and the stench of excrement made it hard to breathe, then deeper into the slums, down the notorious Rookery … and then she was faced with a dead end – the game was up!

She pulled up short, closing her eyes – waiting for the jaws of justice to descend. But then she was being dragged and jerked violently – not backwards but sideways – and she found herself tumbling through a doorway and down damp steps on to a cold stone floor, where a hand was roughly clamped over her mouth and the reticule snatched rudely out of her hands.

It took a moment to register that she was in near-pitch darkness at the bottom of some slimy cellar steps, lying on top of somebody who she could make out only by the sharp gleam of a pair of extremely bright eyes, and by the hand that was clamped over her mouth.

She struggled and gurgled but to no avail.

"Hush, woman, and quit your wrigglin'," urged a whispered voice. "Or you'll 'ave the beaks down here 'an you swingin' in the wind outside Newgate!"

Twill stopped struggling for a moment at the mention of the gallows. She could hear voices above: a clamour of "Where'd she go? … Got clean away … The thief jus' disappeared into thin air!" And the breathless voice of the Doughty Street gentleman declaiming, "My wife's purse ... the little wretch got away with it clean!" followed by the deep tones of a policeman: "Move along, folks ... nothing to see here ... leave it to the law – we'll catch 'er – see if we don't."

Twill stayed very still, suddenly very aware of the loud beating of her heart in the darkness and the hot sharp breaths of her ... rescuer? abductor? ... close to her ear. She felt a huge desire to clamp her teeth down on the hand that was still tightly held over her mouth, but she did not do so till the crowd outside had passed on and the danger was gone.

Then she bit down as hard as she could and as her assailant released her with an angry yell, she turned around and in the gloom beheld ... the top-hatted urchin.

Chapter 13

In which you know who we are going to meet –
don't you?

"**Y**ou!" declared Twill.

The young gentleman before her took a low bow and then looked up with eyes that were full of a rather world-weary mischief.

"Jack Dawkins, miss – at ya service. Some call me John, or Master Dawkins, but generally I am known as the Artful Dodger – or Dodge to me friends. An' I do believe we is goin' to be friends, my good woman!"

"I am not your good woman!" said Twill, hands on hips, eyes ablaze with indignation. "An' I would never be friends with such as you – you nearly had me arrested. Now, give me that reticule so as I can clear my name!"

"What, this?" asked the Artful Dodger.

He was a little older than he had been when he first encountered Twill's brother, all those years ago. A little wiser too. A lad of fifteen – maybe sixteen, for he'd never known his birthday, no more than he had his long-gone parents – and taller now, with an occasional dip and catch to his voice. But the Artful Dodger he was in the flesh, and he dangled the reticule before Twill, who made a sweep for it and missed. Despite the passing of the years, Dodger was as quick as in the days of Fagin's gang – and more wary with it.

"You're a quick 'un, I'll grant you!" said Mr Dawkins. "There's not many can outpace the Artful Dodger. Shame you're not so bright in the upstairs department!" At this he tapped his forehead and raised an eyebrow in a way that made Twill's blood boil.

"Give it here!" said Twill, making another swipe for the reticule. "I need to return it."

"And what you fink'll happened if you does?" said the Dodger. "Turn up at tha' grand house, clutchin' a stolen purse, seekin' a reward, will ya? The traps'll have you clapped in irons an' transported to the colonies – an' tha's if they don't let you swing!"

At this point the Dodger made a pantomime of being suspended by the noose, complete with gurning and gruesome sound effects that were most disconcerting to behold.

Twill paused for a second. "I'll tell them it wasn't me!"

The Dodger just laughed. "You're a green 'un, no mistake! Woutn't 'ave thought it – cos you got a good pair of legs on ya. Though your knowledge of the area ain't wot it needs to be for this line of work. You was lucky I was here to rescue you."

"Rescue me? Of all the nerve! You're the reason I'm in so much trouble."

"Gammon an' spinnage!" said the Dodger, who was, in truth, rather enjoying the encounter with this fair-haired maiden. "Wha's the difference between a rescue and a peachin' job between friends. An' you gotta admit you'da been in a fix without me."

"I've got to admit no such thing!" said Twill. "And if you don't mind – I'll be leaving now."

"Got better places to be, 'ave ya?" said Dodger with an ironic smile. "I woutn't go out there just yet. They'll have peelers stationed all around – on the lookout for you, my flash com-pan-i-on! No, youse best to stay 'ere till it gets dark. Don't fret your eyelids – Dodger'll take care of ya!"

Twill looked outraged but she didn't dare go out and risk arrest.

"Wha's your story then!" asked the Artful Dodger, leaning back against a pile of old crates and surveying Twill with keen interest. There was something familiar about the girl, now that a shaft of light fell down through the cellar door and caught her face in a golden glow. Dodger couldn't quite place it but he was sure he had seen her somewhere before.

"Story?"

Dodger produced a large spotted handkerchief from within his capacious jacket, which he unwrapped to reveal a length of cold sausage. The smell hit Twill's nostrils and her stomach growled with hunger.

"Who are ya? Wha's your name? Where ya from?" asked the Dodger.

"You first!"

"I'm pretty much famous, me," declared Jack Dawkins, removing a small pearl-handled knife from his waistcoat pocket and slicing off a piece of sausage, which he held tantalisingly just out of Twill's reach. "You 'eard of the orphan Oliver Twist, I s'pose?"

Twill had heard of the tale. She and the Camberwell Grove kids had sometimes played it out in the street. She liked to take the role of the gruesome child-snatcher Fagin, or the brave Nancy, who had laid down her life to return the boy to his rightful family, or even

70

the murdering villain Bill Sikes. She didn't recall there being any mention of a top-hatted scoundrel!

"I was the one wot met 'im first!" said Dodger. "When 'e first come to London – all 'ungry and cold, 'e was. It was me wot took 'im to Mr Fagin – you've 'eard of old Fagin, I suppose?"

Twill had indeed. The old wretch, who had run the gang of child thieves, had been sentenced to be hanged outside Newgate – though, according to Mr Scapegrace, he had mysteriously escaped, and no one had heard anything of him since.

"I was Fagin's right-hand man!" declared Dodger proudly. "I 'elped him train Oliver up – tried to, anyhows. He'd never a' made a decent pickpocket – too nervy, too slow. You, on the other hand…"

Dodger surveyed Twill with an admiring glance that made her want to kick him. Dodger grinned, and produced a heel of bread from his tailcoat pocket. "So, you 'ungry, is you?"

Twill shrugged. She did not want to accept anything from this rapscallion of a boy, who had ruined her chances of a respectable career as a kitchen girl. But when he unwrapped some rather musty-looking cheese, which he appeared to be have been storing inside his battered top hat, her stomach betrayed her by rumbling.

"Very well!" said Twill, accepting the bread and sausage and a slice of cheese with very ill grace. And then, because Baggage had taught her it was bad manners not to make conversation at the table, she asked. "What became of Fagin's boys?"

"Don't ya know?" asked Dodger, enjoying Twill's feigned indifference. "After Oliver becomes all la-di-da, he only persuades his guardian that he wants to help unfortunate boys like 'imself, don't he?"

"How did he do that?" asked Twill haughtily, hungrily tucking into the bread.

"The Brownlow Be-nev-o-lent Home for Unfortunate Boys," said Dodger, pronouncing the words with an expression of distaste, as if he were chewing on a snail. "All the boys is taken in, fed an' watered, an' teached up good too."

"Sounds nice?"

"Tha's wha' it's supposed to be. Nice!" Dodger's snub nose wrinkled up as he used the word. "An 'ome for the 'omeless. A refuge for the lost boys. All nice sound-ling like you says…"

"But?" Twill sensed there had been a *but* coming for some time.

Dodger shrugged. "But it weren't the place for me.

Tried it for a bit – liked the vittles an' the new togs they gave us, but the bein' learned – letters and addin' up – ain't no life for a Dodger. I got out of there soon as I could. Back on the streets where a Dodger belongs! It's the life of an adventurer for me!"

The word "adventure" made Twill's heart beat a little faster, but she turned up her nose nonetheless. "What? Stealing things? You call that adventure?"

"I most certainly do!" said Dodger. "Fogles and tickers and ladies' purses – whatever I can get me 'ands on." And with this he produced an array of silk handkerchiefs from his rolled-up sleeves, and proudly withdrew a pocket watch from down the front of his corduroy trousers. "I am an in-de-pen-dent trader now, though. Not answerable to no one. What I steal is me own!"

"Except it's not!" she pointed out. "That purse belonged to the young lady on Doughty Street."

"An' possession is nine tenfs of the law!" declared Dodger. "Ain't you never 'eard that?"

Twill, who had been briefed by Mr Scapegrace in the rudiments of Property Law – young men wagering all their property on the Hazard cards being not unknown at the Black Jack – simply raised her eyebrows.

"So wot about you?" continued Dodger, ignoring

her disdain. "I ain't never see you in this vicinity afore. Wha's your story?"

"Maybe I don't have one!" said Twill, haughtily accepting a second portion of sausage and cheese.

"Everyone 'as a story. An' since we're stuck here for the foreseeable, you might as well share it with old Dodger!"

So Twill narrated the events that had led up to the present, and when she had finished, the Dodger shook his head and offered her the last of the bread, though in truth his own stomach still gaped with hunger. "My eyes! That place sounds like a right bang set-to! Almost as bad as old Fagin, that Manzoni Monster. You're well shut of it!"

"I know, but…" Twill thought of Baggage and a lump rose to her throat.

"Folks like you and me, we is free spirits," said Dodger, wiping crumbs from his face with a pocket handkerchief. "We don't take to being shut up in in-sti-too-tions and the like."

Twill just sniffed and did not look him in the eye.

"You 'aven't nowhere to kip, am I right?" said Dodger, guessing the truth in an instant. "'Ere, I got an idea! I am going to int-er-duce you to some acquaintances of mine wot might be able to assist you."

Twill looked up hopefully.

"But first we gotta get you there wi'out the rozzers catching you," continued Dodger. "Lucky you gots me to 'elp, ain't it?"

Chapter 14

*In which Twill is introduced to the Sassy Sisters
of Saffron Hill and learns that there is honour
among thieves*

It was dark and Twill's heart was beating violently as she and Dodger made their way back into the city streets. Dodger had said there was less chance of being spotted under cover of darkness, and he boasted of knowing every back alley and short cut, so they could avoid the main highways, where there were street lamps and where a top-hatted peeler on the beat might spot Twill and give chase. But still she couldn't stop her heart hammering.

Dodger had said there were other dangers to worry about at night – though he would not say what. The city seemed very different from how it had appeared in the day – bundles of rags in doorways shifted to reveal sleeping figures that moaned like ghosts and made Twill jump, and shapeless figures slunk in dark alleyways from which foul whisperings and the odd inhuman shriek emitted to make her stomach lurch.

As they made their way through Little Saffron Hill and into Saffron-Hill-the-Great, they passed a grubby-looking public house named the Three Cripples, and two drunkards came tumbling out, lurching woozily towards Twill, causing her to cry out in alarm. Dodger grabbed her by the hand and pulled her out of their path.

"You needs to watch you'self," declared Dodger. "You ain't in Camberwell no more!"

Twill shivered a little, annoyed to have shown this boy she was afraid.

But even the Artful Dodger seemed to move with wary urgency now. "Come on – there's eyes in every alleyway hereabouts," he said. "And worse besides!"

Quickening their pace, they hurried on through little-frequented dirty alleyways, which seemed to get narrower and smellier and more maze-like as they delved deeper into the heart of the slums, until at length the Artful stopped before a ramshackle building above which a sign hung drunkenly, declaring, "Price's Printing Press". What had happened to Mr Price was unclear, for the place had the appearance of having been abandoned many years ago. It was a broken and boarded-up skeleton of a building, with chimney stacks leaning drunkenly, and crumbling brickwork that was coated with years of soot and smeared with slime that dripped down the walls, as if the whole place wept for its reduced condition.

"Where are we?" whispered Twill.

But Dodger did not answer – just looked around warily then rapped on the door in a rhythmic "one two, one two, two" pattern. That was when Twill heard the sound of heavy footsteps approaching from the other end of the alleyway. Dodger heard it too. He rapped on the door again, more impatiently this time. The footsteps were getting closer – a heavy tread that reverberated through the night air. Dodge raised his fist to knock again when the door opened just a crack and a low voice whispered, "Cribbage and Rum", to which Mr Jack Dawkins responded, quick as a flash, "Tic-tac-toe – Marco Polo". Then – the footsteps nearly upon them now – a hand reached out and grabbed Dodger. He had the common sense to snatch Twill by the hand, who – for the second time that day – was rudely propelled into an unfamiliar environment.

"What the...?"

But Dodger pressed an urgent finger to Twill's lips and

there was a long moment of held breath as the heavy footfalls passed right by the doorway – pausing just for a second – before moving on. During this interlude Twill's eyes adjusted to the gloom, and she was able to make out a large warehouse that had once been used for Price's trade. It was lit by only a few tallow candles, so she could just make out a giant rusted printing press in the middle of the floor and some other paraphernalia rusting in damp corners. Instead of being filled with printed pages, however, the place was bedecked with what looked like pocket handkerchiefs, hung out to dry like a laundry. There were other trinkets besides: Twill spotted a lady's parasol in soft grey silk, a mantle of fox fur, a dozen or so pocket watches which hung by a rusty old furnace, and – was that a set of intimate undergarments strung across one of the boarded-up windows?

"That were a close one!" said Dodger – but he wasn't addressing her, for in the corners of this vast damp space Twill now saw there lurked a dozen or so young ladies, if that be the correct term for them, scattered about like the rubbish dumped on Mount Pleasant. And all of them were now staring intently at her.

"Why ya comin' 'ere this time a' night, Dodger?" demanded a red-headed wench – presumably the one who had answered the door and dragged them inside.

"An' a very good evenin' to you too, my dear Chelsea," said Dodger, with a low bow and a flourish.

"Was you followed?" demanded the young lady, who was taller than Twill but perhaps not much older, with a wiry frame and a face that might have been described as handsome if she didn't look so cross. "Did the Child Catchers spy you comin' 'ere?"

"Don't fret your eyelids, my little Chelsea bun." (This made the red-headed maiden flush the same colour as her hair). "The traps ain't followed me, and there was no sign of the Child Catchers neither. I brung along a new acquaintance, is all."

The red-haired maiden called Chelsea turned to look at Twill as the other girls edged closer, emerging from dark corners, whispering and staring – half a dozen sets of wide eyes taking in Twill's almost-clean apron and her almost-clean fingernails, both of which stood in stark contrast to any of their own.

"Who's ya lady friend, Dodger?" demanded a young girl of maybe eight or nine, with one eye folded permanently shut, like a round white moon in her dirty rose of a face.

"An' what you bringin' a posh cove like that 'ere for?" asked one of a pair of stocky-looking twins with identical squashed noses that looked as if they had been broken and mended several times each.

"Ladies, let's play nice and remember our manners!" said Dodger. Then he turned to Twill and announced with aplomb, "Miss Twill Jones, meet the Sassy Sisters of Saffron Hill! An all-female crew of vagabonds, thieves, prigs an' down-an'-out bad 'uns."

"An' the best in the business!" added the second of the broken-nose twins.

"The Sisterhood is an independent venture, based on democratic and Amazonian principles," Dodger continued.

"What we steal we share," declared a rather pungent young lady with an expression as belligerent as a bare-knuckle fighter. "No one takes a cut, no one tells us what do to, nor pushes us around."

"And the most important rule of all," declared Chelsea, evidently the leader of the pack. "No men – no boys – girls only!"

"Exceptin' me!" declared the Dodger with another sweeping bow. "I am an honourable exception. An honorary sister. Ain't that right, ladies!"

"If you means youse a big girl's blouse, then that's about right!" Chelsea emitted a loud sniff and continued to eye Twill with angry suspicion. "An' you'd better have summat good in them pockets o' yours, comin' 'ere this time a night, or the girls'll sling you back out for the child snatchers to take!"

"Come now, Miss Chelsea, you woutn't do that to your dear old Dodge!" said Dodger, taking her hand and bestowing a delicate kiss, which elicited an eruption of giggling from the younger girls, who now crowded round and tugged at his pockets, revealing several handkerchiefs and the large golden pocket watch Dodger had shown Twill earlier, as well as the remaining sausage and the young lady's reticule.

"Ooh – where'd you get this ticker, Dodge?" asked the girl with the closed eye.

"Why, young Sloane, from a prime plant up by Pembroke Gardens," said Dodger with a grin. "There's rich pickin's that way now all the la-di-das been moving in – ruining the area, if you ask me!"

"An' what about this pretty purse?" asked a tiny tot of a girl – the smallest of them all – with skin the colour of warm chocolate and eyes as blue as periwinkles.

Dodger bent down to pick up the tiny mite and sling her up on to his hip. "From a Doughty Street dame, but I nearly had to fight this one for it." He indicated Twill with a jerk of this thumb. "Had a chase on my hands, so I did, young Angel!"

The little girl stared at Twill with undisguised admiration and all the other girls surveyed her with surprise. Only Chelsea continued to scowl.

"Caught the Dodger, did ya?" she asked.

"Yes," said Twill, meeting the challenge in that young lady's eye without blinking. "An' then he stitched me up – like a louse!"

"I foxed you, is all!" said Dodger. "Showed I was the superior tactician. Then saved your life!"

"If that's what you want to tell yourself!"

Ignoring this slight, Dodger turned back to the cherubic-looking creature balanced on his knee. "Look what else I managed to catch, young Angel!" He gave the young girl a twist of paper, and she opened it with an "ooh" of delight.

"Sugar mice, Dodger!" she exclaimed. "Look at their tiny noses!"

"Where'd you get 'em, Dodge?" asked one of the twins. Twill noticed that each girl had one brown eye and one green, the only difference being that the colours were reversed, so that if they stood side by side they were in perfect symmetry.

"I pur-loined them from that doddery old sweet seller on Clerkenwell Green," said Dodge. "Half blind 'e is – never saw me comin'!"

There was something about the way he said this that made Twill think he wasn't being entirely truthful, though she couldn't imagine why.

"Oh, Dodge!" said Angel, wrapping her little arms around his neck and planting a kiss on his grubby cheek. "You're the best!"

Twill was surprised to see Mr Jack Dawkins blush.

"Enough of this twaddle!" barked Chelsea. "Let's introduce ourselves to Dodger's new acquaintance!"

All the young ladies, it transpired, were named after the places they had been found before they came to Price's Printing Press. There was Battersea, a squat-looking girl with the appearance of a pugilistic pug; Sloane, whose half-closed eye and scarred cheek had been gained in an encounter with the Old Bill on the King's Road; Fleet, whose feet proved to be as fast as her name implied and who was as grubby and pungent as that river tributary itself; Chelsea, who had slept a whole winter in the snow on Eaton Terrace; and little Angel, who had been found starving on a street corner in Islington. Poor Piccadilly and Trafalgar – the symmetrical twins – seemed to have come off worst from the naming strategy, but as Chelsea pointed out, "None of us got no call to be ashamed of where we

84

come from!"

"And I am but an 'umble conduit for the Sassy Sisterhood," said the Dodger. "I broker certain deals for the resale of the – ahem – vintage goods these ladies procure."

"You're a fence!" said Twill, who was familiar with the term for one who launders and sells on stolen goods too hot to handle. Occasionally, Mr Scapegrace did dealings with such gentlemen in the back offices of the Black Jack for reasons that did no credit to that establishment.

"A vulgar term," said Dodger, pretending to look offended. "I am an en-tre-pren-ure, helping these good ladies turn the sweat of their labours to 'ard blunt!"

The small girl called Angel had slipped her hand into Twill's and was now looking up at her with bright eyes. "You looks 'ungry, miss!" she declared. "We got bacon – an' broth too – an' sugar mice what the dear old Dodger cadged for us. Want some?"

In truth, Twill was starving hungry again. It seemed like days since she had eaten the bread and cheese with Dodger, though it was in truth no more than a few hours. But Chelsea was still eyeing her suspiciously, and Twill was far from sure that she was welcome in the Sisterhood.

"Well," said Dodger, turning to the flame-haired leader of the clan. "You got room for one more?"

"Can she pull her weight?" demanded Chelsea.

"She's as speedy on her pins as you could wish for!" said Dodger. "I can vouch for that!"

"An' she won't peach?"

"She'll be dark as a safe," said the Dodger. "I knew it the first moment I clapped eyes on 'er. Said to meself, there's a gal wot you can trust."

Chelsea looked from Dodger to Twill then back again, as if trying to decide something. All the other girls waited for her verdict – and Twill was surprised to realise that she wanted to stay. Despite their rags and grubby faces, there was something about this clan that reminded her of the female camaraderie of the Butterfly boudoir.

"Please, Chelsea!" said little Angel, with plaintive eyes.

Chelsea sighed and gave a non-committal shrug. "She can stay for tonight and then we'll see."

Angel emitted a squeal of delight.

"What we callin' you then?" demanded Chelsea.

"Oh, she's a south of the river girl!" said Dodger with a giant grin. "Camberwell, ditn't you say? Nice – suits you, I reckons."

"My name," said Twill, sticking out her chin and casting a disdainful look at the Dodger, "is Twill Jones."

Chapter 15

*In which Twill proves her sass and Dodger pays
the price for a kiss*

C helsea declared that Twill's continued tenure at
the printing press was dependent on her proving
that she had the skills of the Sisterhood, and so the next
morning, along with Angel and Dodger, she took Twill
out to teach her the tricks of the trade. "Gotta prove
you're up to scratch," Sloane had explained to her over
a breakfast of bread and warm milk. "If you wants to
stay, that is!"

"Every sister brings some blunt to the table," added
Battersea. "That's how it works."

Twill nodded. She had slept surprisingly soundly,
on a mattress of old rags and newspapers beneath
the skeleton of the old printing press, with little Angel
pressed up tight next to her, smelling of coal soap and

sugar mice, and she had awoken surprisingly excited – and nervous – about the day's adventures ahead.

"Gotta fink of yourself like that Robin Hood," added Dodger, who had reappeared at dawn, bringing with him a bunch of rather battered carnations, allegedly purloined from a Covent Garden flower seller, which he distributed to each of the girls, causing much delight.

"What do you mean?" asked Twill. The flowers had not impressed her as much as they had the younger Sisters.

"Why, cos we is robbin' from the rich to give t' the poor," said the pungent young lady called Fleet.

"The poor?"

"Tha's us!" said Dodger.

"An' all the Sisters," said Angel. "Dodger says we are like the band of merry men – only girls! Merry girls!"

"Ex-act-ly!" said Dodge. "It's redistribution of wealth. The government oughta be thanking us for it."

Twill wondered what her beloved Baggage would make of her choice of new occupation. The life of a pickpocket was certainly not what Baggage Jones had in mind for her ... but then she had made Twill promise not to return. Which meant she would have to find a new occupation – and a new place to live – if she could prove that she was up to it.

89

She was pondering how she might do so as they made their way through Smithfield Market, where they were confronted with the wall of odour from the slaughtered pigs. The steam rising from the recently despatched carcasses mingled with the vapour rising from the horse dung and made Twill gag.

"Come on, Camberwell!" said Dodger, wrinkling his face. "Afore me nose drops off cos a the smell!"

Then down they went through Little Britain, past St Bart's hospital, through the square that Dodger told her was haunted. "Some lady queen – long time ago – built a giant bonfire here an' burned a load of old priests for sport," he told her. "Sat up there, they say." He indicated a small window above the entrance to the old Tudor church of St Bartholomew.

Twill felt herself shiver in the dank and murky morning air. She could almost feel the breath of the ghosts hovering about her. But this was no time for cold feet and bogey tales. Chelsea had explained the importance of picking out your "mark" – and as they made their way past the ancient church of St Bart's, Dodger pointed out a flamboyantly dressed young gentleman with an elaborately tied neckcloth, shirt points starched so high he looked like he could barely breathe, and a waistcoat of a violent salmon colour that clashed horribly with his overly tight camel hessians. The young gentleman was berating a young flower seller angrily over the price of a bunch of violets.

"Just the man!" said Chelsea. "Your challenge is to relieve that gentleman of 'is pocket watch."

Over the years, the Butterflies had taught Twill the tricks of their trade – how to use nimble sleight of hand to slip rings from fingers; pocket watches from chains; coins from the deepest of pockets – for Madam Manzoni insisted that her girls learn to rob the customers blind in as many ways as possible. But this – on the streets of London in broad daylight – was a different matter altogether.

"Allow me to assist," said Dodger, slipping his arm though Twill's in a most presumptuous manner. "You just need to act like youse in love wiv me."

"What?" Twill exclaimed.

"Shoutn't be too hard!" said Dodger, tugging her in the direction of the flower seller. "You just gaze into my eyes…"

Twill shot a fiery glance in his direction, which could hardly have been described as loving.

"Then when I goes in for a kiss, you grabs the ticker!" Twill ground to a sudden halt. "You wouldn't dare!"

"Oh, woutn't I, South o' th' River?" said the Dodger,

who appeared to be enjoying the charade far more than Twill considered seemly.

"Just you try and you'll find yourself in that pile of pigswill over there!" Twill indicated to a farmer driving his hogs down to Smithfield Market.

Dodger just grinned, undaunted by the threat. They were closer to their mark now, and as Twill heard the gentleman berating the old flower seller in the vilest terms, she felt a flash of anger on behalf of the poor defenceless woman, and a sudden desire to see Pink Waistcoat get his just deserts.

"Fine!" she said to Dodger. "I'll do it, but my way – don't you try nothing funny!"

She could see Angel and Chelsea on the other side of the street, keeping a lookout for the long arm of the law, and she wondered if Dodger tried this particular tactic with all the girls.

She positioned herself close to the pink waistcoat, who smelled of a sickly sweet *eau de cologne*, surveying his salmon-pink bulk and contemplating the best way to relieve him of his possessions. But before she had a chance to put any such property redistribution plan into action, she felt an arm around her waist and heard Dodger declare, "Here goes, my pretty one!" and then he was pulling her close and puckering his lips in a most alarming manner. Luckily Twill's reflexes were as quick as Mr Dawkins', and she had unhooked his presumptuous arm and slapped him on his puckered face before she'd managed to get out the words, "How dare you – unhand me, sir!"

"But I loves you with all me 'eart, me darlin'!" Dodger declaimed, lunging enthusiastically for a second embrace.

An indignant Twill staggered back towards Pink Waistcoat, who was blurting something about "unmannerly youths" and "young ruffians". Across the road Angel and Chelsea were in fits of giggles but, recalling what she was here for, Twill turned to grab Pink Waistcoat, clutching him for protection, crying, "Oh, help me, good sir!" while slipping her hand into his pocket to relieve him of his timepiece – and his wallet at the same time.

"Unhand me, woman!" Pink Waistcoat declared, shoving her backwards into the arms of the Artful Dodger, who took advantage of Twill's momentary discomposure to plant a kiss upon her protesting lips.

Red-faced and fuming, Twill turned round and slapped his grinning face, declaring to both Pink Waistcoat and Dodger, "All men are pigs!" before storming off around the corner, with Dodger following, begging for forgiveness – and the pink man's loot in her apron pocket.

Once out of sight of the flower seller, all four of them ran hell for leather, not stopping till they reached the Strand, where they ducked into an alleyway by the old Roman Baths, far enough from the scene of the crime for them all to safely catch their breaths.

"That," panted Chelsea, "was better than the Covent Garden opera show."

"You looked so very cross when Dodger kissed you, Twill!" giggled young Angel.

"She's a great actress!" said Dodger, surveying Twill with an impish grin. "She loved it really!"

"I most certainly did not – and if you EVER try a stunt like that again," said Twill, "I'll … I'll…" She did not have the words for the damage she intended to inflict upon Dodger's person, but the look in her eye was dangerous enough to convey her intentions.

"You got the loot?" said Chelsea.

Twill turned away from Dodger's maddening grin, reached into her apron pocket and proudly produced a timepiece, a well-lined wallet and a silken handkerchief of salmon pink.

"Not bad," said the red-haired leader of the Sassy Sisterhood.

"So," asked Twill apprehensively. "Am I in?"

Chelsea gave a loud sniff, then shrugged non-committally. "I s'pose you can stay if you wants."

"What did I tell you, girls!" said Dodger. "She's a natural."

Chapter 16

*In which we learn that a leopard who changes his
name does not change his spots*

"You are officially a member of the Saffron Hill
Sisters, young Camberwell!" said Dodger
after the other two headed back with their loot to the
printing press. Angel tired easily – though she would
never admit it – and had only agreed to return when
Chelsea said her own feet were sore, and with a promise
from Dodger that he would filch some cinder toffee
from the sweet seller if she did.

"So I'm gonna give you a tour of the top pickin'
districts!"

Dodger produced a couple of rosy red apples from
his capacious coat pockets and handed one to Twill as
they made their way through the bewildering array
of quadrangles, gardens and courtyards that made up

Middle Temple and Clifford's Inn.

"The Artful Dodger's top-secret tips for pickpocketing pleasure."

"Why are you showing me, if they're so secret?" demanded Twill, still not prepared to forgive him for his assault upon her honour.

"I need t' pass on the knowledge for when I'm gone," said Dodger.

"Gone?" said Twill. "Where are you going?"

"I'm finking of moving to pastures new," said Dodger. "Get meself passage on one of them ships to the New World – America, Canada – I don't much mind where. I missed out on a trip to Botany Bay a little while back, an' ever since then I got itchy feet an' a longin' to see the world, you unnerstand?"

"I do," said Twill, a little wistfully.

"Besides, old Lunnun town is a-changing," said Dodger, biting into his apple as they passed a pair of bewigged lawyers, who surveyed them with haughty stares. "An' these streets is getting a little too hot for me. Ever since the Chief Child Catcher an' his band of kiddy-nappers took to the streets, things has started a-changing."

"Child Catchers?" said Twill, recalling that both Dodger and Chelsea had used the phrase last night.

"Who are they?"

"You really ain't never 'eard of the Child Catchers?" said Dodger in surprise. They had stopped by a sweet stall and Dodger was handing over a ha'penny for a bag of cinder toffee – all quite above board – though Twill imagined Angel would hear a more dastardly version of the transaction later.

"You south of the river types don't know much, do ya?" said Dodger, pocketing the sweets with a wink in her direction. "The Child Catchers are only the most sinister monsters to haunt the streets of London since there was mammoths and sabretooth tigers prowlin' along the banks o' the Thames."

"They sound like bogey men!" said Twill, pulling a face and looking at him in disbelief. "Are they real?"

"Real as this hat!" declared Dodger.

And, as if to prove the veracity of Dodger's words, at that very moment, the Chief Child Catcher himself decided to make an appearance in our tale.

The intrepid pair of pickpockets were, by this time, near the location of the Brownlow Benevolent Home for Unfortunate Boys. Dodger had pointed out the place, and, for some reason, standing in its shadow, Twill felt a chill go down her spine. The grey walls of this austere institution rose towards the early morning smog, and the dark black gates, above which the name of the institution was wrought in iron, seemed to Twill to look more like a prison entrance than a place of refuge.

Just as they were about to step into the square in front of this benevolent institution there appeared a stout barrel of a man, dressed in what looked like a mixture of scarlet regimentals and a bishop's cloak. This extraordinary uniform strained over his elephantine form, bulging over a mountainous belly, which hovered precariously over a pair of incongruously slender legs, clad in whitest hessian and highly polished buckskin boots. This remarkable get-up was topped off with a voluminous tricorn hat and a large golden chain of office, which clanked around the man's neck.

"The Chief Child Catcher!" hissed Dodger, grabbing Twill by the arm and pulling her into the shadow of an alleyway where they could not be seen.

Twill stared at the leader of this mythical band of creatures with interest. She couldn't help feeling that he looked oddly familiar. His face was bulbous and red, and he huffed and puffed as he walked, like an old steam engine. He carried himself with such an air of importance, beaming down at the populace as he proceeded towards the doors of the Benevolent Home, and yet something about him made Twill shudder.

"Not often you see 'im bring one in 'isself," Dodger observed, referring presumably to the ragged bundle of misery that the corpulent gentleman was leading, shivering, towards the gates.

"Poor kid!" muttered Dodger. "Nowt we can do for 'im now though!"

They watched as another young boy unlocked the gates. He was not much less ragged and pale-looking than the Chief Child Catcher's prisoner – in fact, he was so pale he almost seemed to glow blue in the morning mist. Behind him there appeared a hooded figure, bent and crooked, with a hat pulled low and a kerchief wrapped over their face to cover their features. This shadowy being shook the Chief Child Catcher by the hand and the two appeared to exchange a few words.

"Who's that?" whispered Twill.

Dodger was staring hard at the gnarled figure, a puzzled expression on his face. "Ain't seen 'im before. Must be the new overseer the boys been tellin' me 'bout."

Dodger strained to get a closer look, but the crooked figure kept his hood low, muttering words too softly for the onlookers to hear, before the portly gent and his shivering charge were admitted, the gates clanged ominously shut, and the three disappeared from view.

"I thought you said the Benevolent Home for Unfortunate Boys was set up to *help* street urchins," said Twill when they'd gone. Dodger was leaning back against the grimy brickwork, wrapped in thought. "Feed 'em, clothe 'em, teach 'em – that's what you said."

"An' that's what it was," said Dodge, frowning and shaking his head. "But things 'as changed since the Child Catchers took to the streets."

Twill was puzzled. "You keep saying that, but who exactly *are* the Child Catchers?"

"Oh, it's all fine an' above board," said Dodger, rolling his eyes. "Mr Brownlow 'isself was behind settin' 'em up. The police knows about it – parliament too, no doubt. They all applaud the old gent for his benevolence!"

Twill saw that Dodger was eyeing a pocket watch that dangled tantalisingly from the waistcoat of a dandy-looking young man who passed by, though he chose not to relieve him of it.

"Course, they don't call 'em Child Catchers," Dodger continued. Then he adopted a stance and tone like he was the prime minister himself. "They is called the Commission for the Location and Rescue of Vagrant Children – or summat high-falutin' like that. An' that old gent dressed up like a giant strawberry puff back there – 'e was the head commissioner. Bumble by name."

Bumble by name, beadle by former profession, blackguard and scoundrel as he will be known to readers of the tale of Oliver Twist. Yes, this was he. One and the same Mr Bumble who – so many years before – had cast Twill out into the snow, sold Oliver for an undertaker's apprentice, then consorted with his dastardly half-brother to rob the boy of his inheritance. Yet now he had apparently shaken off the stain of that association and risen up in the eyes of the world once again.

"Bumble?" said Twill. "Where have I heard that name before?"

"A greater scoundrel you couldn't 'ope to meet!" said Dodger feelingly. "But 'e persuaded Mr Brownlow 'e'd seen the light, seen the error of 'is ways, said he wanted to do penance for the harm 'e'd caused young Oliver by rescuin' others like him!"

"And does he?"

"Not likely! 'Im and 'is Child Catchers scour the streets for lost boys, homeless young fellows in need of a bed for the night an' a good meal."

"And then they take them – to the Benevolent Home for Unfortunate Boys?"

"Eggs-actly! But things ain't what they was since Mr Brownlow fell sick," said Dodger. "None of the old gang hung around once things started a-changing. They said them that is runnin' the place now ain't got such al-true-istic motives as the good old man."

"That hooded gentleman? Who is he?"

"The boys call 'im the Old Devil," said Dodger, shaking his head and frowning. "He names hisself Mr Barrabas. Appointed last month by the Strawberry Puff hisself, an' the two of them is thick as thieves. Nobody knows who 'e is, nor where 'e came from. Appeared from nowhere, keeps close in the walls of the Benevolent – but there's something about him…" Dodger looked perplexed again. "I don't know what it is." He fell silent for a moment, as if trying to puzzle out a mystery that lay just out of his grasp. "An' there's a bad change afoot in the place too!" he went on.

"What sort of change?"

"I don't know for sure," said the Dodger. "Can't get near the old place no more. Used to pop in for a bite to eat if business was slow, but now they got locks on the gates – not sure if it's to keep the boys in or the pryin' eyes out. But I got my spies. I'll find out what that crooked gent is up to – see if I don't."

Chapter 17

*In which some time passes and Twill learns a
dubious trade and embraces Sisterhood*

Twill soon settled in to the Sassy Sisterhood.
Within a week she felt like one of the family.
Within two, she could barely imagine any other life
than that of the streets. And within a month, she was
one of the most accomplished dippers and pocket-
pickers between Highgate and High Holborn.

Unlike her twin brother, whose delicate sensibilities
had made him unsuited to a life of petty thievery and
pickpocketery, Twill was quick-thinking and fleet-of-
foot. Moreover, her time at the Black Jack had given
her a dim view of rich folks and the feudal principles
on which the laws of England were founded – the
belief that those who *have* deserve what they have, and
those who *have-not* deserve no better. On the contrary,

Twill believed that those who possessed far more than they needed should share with those who went cold and hungry for want of having enough. And if they had to be encouraged to share their wealth with a little assistance from small hands dipped into pockets, then that was just the good lord's way of achieving equality on earth.

If Twill sometimes shared her brother's moral qualms about thievery, she contented herself by only picking targets who were thoroughly objectionable: a middle-aged woman draped in pearls who beat her little dog with a stick; an elderly gentleman with rings on every finger whom she overheard telling his son he was and always would be a grave disappointment. Such specimens Twill felt deserved what life handed to them – and what Twill could take away.

The only thing that occasioned Twill a twinge of guilt at the line of work she had turned her hand to was the knowledge that Baggage had wanted better for her. Baggage had insisted that she learn to read and write, taught her to cook and manage a home, and had dreamed of Twill rising from kitchen maid to housekeeper of some grand establishment. She had certainly not wanted her girl to be a common thief, living in the same rubbish heap from which Baggage had picked her up.

But Baggage had also told her never to return. And Twill knew there was no way she could. She had run away from Madam Manzoni – and to return would invite who knew what dire punishments upon her head.

So Twill threw herself into her new line of work. She and the Sisters took to the streets each day, in pairs or small groups, varying their locations to avoid detection, doing their bit to even out the inequities of wealth in the capital. And Twill soon came to know all the sights of London – the bewigged lawyers of Lincoln's Inn; the opera crowd in Covent Garden; the surgeons of St Bart's; and the meat-mongers of Smithfield Market. And she came to love the life of a ragamuffin adventurer. It wasn't quite the same as venturing to the Indies, or sailing the China Seas, rounding the Cape or trekking through the plains of Africa, but it was a long way from Camberwell Grove.

She had also found a new family of sorts. The Sassy Sisters were a funny, assorted bunch – a bit like the Butterflies in some ways, although younger on average and more ragged in appearance. But the main difference lay in their freedom. The Sisters worked for themselves – and for each other. They served no master or mistress. What they stole was theirs if they chose to keep it, though they all chose to share. From the tiniest mite like Angel to big bruisers like Sloane – even the twins, Piccadilly and Trafalgar, who sometimes spoke to each other in their own secret language that no one else understood – they all shared. And they were beholden to no one.

And yet Twill still missed the Black Jack with a yawning ache. The Butterflies, the boudoir, lessons with Mr Scapegrace, even the sound of the young gentlemen throwing away their fortunes and carousing raucously all hours of the day and night. Most of all she missed her Baggage. Missed her as it might feel to miss your heart if it was no longer beating in your chest, or your leg if it had been eaten by a shark. But she had promised not to return and she was determined to keep her promise.

And perhaps Twill might have settled in and made a life for herself with the Sisters had it not been for the Child Catchers. For each day since that first sighting of the Chief Child Catcher, Twill heard more and more tales of orphaned wretches snatched from the streets. Each time one of the girls took her out, they told her to be on her guard against the Old Bill, the magistrates – but most of all the Child Catchers. For though it was boys they targeted, Chelsea said you could never be too careful.

"There might be cases of mistaken id-en-tity," she said, glancing at Fleet – who did indeed look more like a boy than a young lady. "An' anyways, who knows when they might start targeting girls!"

Dodger was an erratic but frequent visitor to the Sassy Sisters, turning up sometimes every day, sometimes not for days on end. And if some of the Sisters observed that his visits had been more frequent since the arrival of Miss Twill Jones, none had the temerity to say this out loud.

It was maybe three or four months after her arrival at the Sisterhood – the time had flown so fast she couldn't remember rightly any more – when Dodger arrived on the doorstep of Price's Printing Press at barely five o'clock in the morning. It was Twill who answered the door, still bleary-eyed from sleep, to find Dodger shrouded in mist with a dark look on his face. "Come on, South o' th' River," he commanded in a low whisper. "Youse comin' with me!"

Twill knew him well enough by now not to enquire further. She tiptoed back to the rag mattress she shared with little Angel, tucking the blanket over the small girl's sleeping form and pulling a thin shawl over her own shoulders, before making her way out into the grey London dawn.

"Where are we going?" she whispered, closing the door quietly so as not to disturb the sleeping girls.

"I need to check up on somefing," said Dodger. "New intelligence 'as come in – of a most alarmin' nature."

"Intelligence from who?"

"One of my men in the field!" said Dodger, pulling Twill into a nook near White Horse Alley. They were just off Field Lane, in the area known as the Rookery – one of the worst slums in London, where squalid dwellings bred disease and crime and misery faster than the rats that fed on them.

A whistle emitted from nearby – one sharp blast and two longs ones.

Dodger put two fingers between his lips and copied the whistle – one short blast, two long ones – and in an instant a small boy appeared, like a miniature ghost from the morning mist, and stood before them. He was wearing the same drab uniform as the urchin who had opened the gate to the Brownlow Benevolent Home for Unfortunate Boys, but his was stained bluey-black, as was his skin and his hair. In fact, the plum-coloured state of his whole appearance gave him the look of a bruise.

"All right, Dodger!" he said, looking round shiftily.

"Who's the gal?"

"Miss Twill Jones, meet Tommy Tickle," said Dodger. "Late inhabitant of the Benevolent Home and erstwhile street urchin and pocket-dipper of the first order."

"Pleased to meet you," said Twill, extending a hand.

"Likewise, miss!" said Tommy Tickle, shaking hers most vigorously with a small, mottled-blue paw. "Any lady friend of Dodger is a friend of ours. 'E's got good taste in the fillics, 'as Dodger!"

"I am not his 'lady friend'!" protested Twill. "I'm not even sure I would call us friends."

"Give it time," said Dodger, winking at Tommy Tickle in a manner that enraged Twill and caused young Master Tickle to emit a gurgling chuckle.

"Mr Tickle here lately absconded from the Benevolent," said Dodger. "Made a break for it last night, ditn't you, Tom?"

"I did, Dodge. None too easy it was neither. Tighter than old Newgate Prison, the place is now. Plenty o' new boys comin' in but none's seein' the light of day again."

"You done well to get out yisself, young Tickle."

"You know me, Dodge!" said Master Tickle proudly.

111

"I coutn't stay there no longer. Not 'ow things are nowadays."

"Things aren't what they were?" asked Twill.

"No, miss! Since the old devil Barrabas takes over runnin' the place it's all changed," said Tommy, shaking his head lamentably. "The food's worse for one. No better 'an workhouse fare – gruel twice a day an' a portion a' bread and butter on Sundays, if we's lucky."

"You'll be wanting this then," said Dodger, producing from his pocket a somewhat musty-looking sausage and a quarter loaf, which Tommy Tickle grabbed eagerly.

"I for one don't miss the schoolin' – readin' and writin' an' that," said Tommy, through a mouthful of sausage and bread. "But there's 'em who does."

"No lessons at all now?" said Twill.

Tommy Tickle shook his head. Twill noticed that even his flaxen locks were tinged with the same distinctive blue colour, and she recalled the same violet tone she had spotted on the boy who had opened the gates to Bumble all those weeks ago. "The Old Devil – that's Mr Barrabas, miss – 'e says we got to pay our way now, see. Says we can't scrounge off society forever. Gotta prove ourselves profitable citizens."

"Profitable? Why, what do they have you do?" asked Twill.

"Come wi' me, miss!" said young Mr Tickle, his face looking bluer than ever as the weak morning light struggled its way through the layers of smog that hung over the city. "I'll show you."

Chapter 18

*In which Twill sees evidence of man's
inhumanity to man*

Round the back of the austere grey walls of the Benevolent, down an alley, through a small courtyard and ducking through a rickety old fence, the trio came to a small weeded area where, by contorting into a crevasse in the brickwork they could peer through a tiny window into a basement below. Tommy crawled down first then indicated that Twill should follow.

"Come an' look. It'll do your eyes a mischief though, be warned."

Twill shuffled on her belly, levering her body on her elbows so that she was able to peer through the tiny pane of grimy glass. Her eyes had to adjust to the gloom, and to the bleary pane and the steam that seemed to fill the basement into which she was looking, but as they did, her blood ran cold.

She beheld a damp cellar, in the centre of which were huge vats of bubbling black liquid, emitting the clouds of purple and grey smoke that filled the room. Among this sea of violet fug, small figures scurried like rats. Children. Some of these ragged creatures stood with giant ladles, stirring the hell-broth liquid, cloths tied tight around their faces, though this did not prevent them coughing as they breathed in the noxious fumes. Some were employed feeding shovelfuls of coal into giant furnaces, which burned in one corner of the room. Others were bent under the burden of buckets sloshing with the black tar-like substance, which they carried from the vats to the smelting pots to the long tables. On these were laid out ceramic jars into which yet more children decanted the liquid. Others sealed lids on to the pots with wax while still more were sticking on labels with glue. Even through the mist, Twill could see that many of these small figures bore the scars of their encounters with the scalding infusion.

This whole scene was presided over by a bent-looking figure in a hood with a hat pulled low over his brow, and a kerchief obscuring all but his eyes, who barked at the mites to "Move faster, my dears ... keep up the pace ... hurry, hurry, hurry, my dears. We don't have all day, you know!", while rubbing his hands together at the sight of the crates of jars stacking up higher and higher by the cellar door.

"What is this place?" said Twill in a horrified whisper.

"An underground blacking factory is what it is!" said Tommy. "Nobody knows it's 'ere save Mr Barrabas hisself and the Child Catchers."

Twill glanced at Dodger, who was uncharacteristically silent, staring into the pit with a grim expression on his face.

"The Old Devil!" murmured Dodger, his eyes still fixed on the scene in front of him, and most particularly on the bent and masked figure in the centre.

"The blacking?" said Twill, covering her mouth with her hand – for the noxious fumes seeped out through the tiny pane of glass, making her lungs feel tight and burning. "It's – horrible!"

"I's meant for shinin' the posh gents' trotter cases – that's shoes, to you an' me," said Tommy knowledgeably. "But the stuff gets in your lungs, in your eyes, your skin. Look at me – I'm the colour of a bobby's jacket. Ain't never gonna see my white skin never again. Some of the lads 'ave started coughin' summat terrible. An' blue blood it is they cough up, miss!"

Twill surveyed the purplish hue of Tommy, who,

besides looking distinctly undernourished, had a smell of sickness about him that reminded Twill of a time when a former Butterfly named Birdy had contracted an infection of the lungs, resulting in her dismissal from the Black Jack.

"An' some's got burns from the scaldin' liquid," Tommy went on. "Little Joe nearly lost an eye last week when the cauldron started spittin'."

Dodger growled beneath his breath and Twill could see his eyes were ablaze.

"But this is awful!" said Twill. "Why don't the boys just leave?"

But the question was merely rhetorical. For presiding over the scene was the looming figure of the Old Devil, or Mr Barrabas, or whatever his name was. Crooked and bent, he moved through the dusky gloom pointing a shrivelled finger or slamming his stick and wheedling, cajoling the boys to keep going.

"Such nice work, my pretty ones," Twill heard him croon. "You make Mr Brownlow so proud!"

And as he spoke he pulled down the kerchief for a second and she caught sight of the long skeletal face, the rascally smile beneath a pair of thick red eyebrows.

"Satan himself!" exclaimed Dodger, the look of intense fury in his eyes now magnified a thousand-fold.

"Returned from the hot place below where he belongs!"

"Do you know him?" asked Twill.

"Curse the day I set eyes on his demon face again," said Dodger. "I know 'im all too well."

Chapter 19

*In which an old adversary returns from the
shadow of the gallows*

Yes, reader, you too have guessed the truth. You too know this devilish old man all too well. He might now go by the name of Mr Barrabas and the boys might call him the Old Devil, but the man whose return coincided so neatly with the transformation of the Benevolent Home for Unfortunate Boys from heaven to hell was none other than the notorious Mr Fagin.

How so? I hear you ask. How can this be? I hear you shudder. And I echo your gasp, I share your wonderment. For wasn't Mr Fagin – former ringleader of the gang of child-thieves to whom Dodger belonged and who had kidnapped young Oliver from the streets – wasn't he sentenced to hang at the end of the story of young Master Twist? Wasn't he last seen about to mount the gallows outside Newgate Prison? In truth, dear reader, you must forgive the gaps in this narrative, for indeed nobody knows how Fagin managed to escape hanging or who helped orchestrate the plot to break him free from prison and make him "disappear". There was talk – of course! Some said he paid off the bellman from St Sepulchre-without-Newgate – the church that overlooked the gallows' square. Some talked of a secret underground passageway through which old Fagin was smuggled at midnight. Some said another unfortunate soul dressed in his clothes swung from the gallows the next morning to entertain the crowds who gathered to watch the spectacle.

But this is all rumour and speculation, for nobody knows for certain how he absconded, nor where he escaped to. Nobody – not even the spinner of this narrative – can tell where he has been for the past few years, nor what he has been up to. Some say he's been off in the Indies, some say China – others says Essex. Whatever the truth, Mr Fagin has returned, with a clean new name, and, what's more, he seems indeed to have inveigled his way into the running of the Benevolent Home which, as Twill had lately witnessed, he now ran in a more nefarious manner even than the den of thieves to which Dodger himself had once belonged. The only difference now was that Mr Fagin did so with the cover of respectability and enjoying the full protection of the law.

All this Master Tommy conveyed to Twill in somewhat garbled form, while Dodger continued to stare in blazing silence.

"So the Child Catchers are in on it too?" asked Twill, still horrified by the sight of the dozens of blue-stained urchins working in the basement hell, presided over by the devil himself.

"Course they are!" said Tommy, who was enjoying the superiority that his inside knowledge gave him. "Big Bumble – the Chief Child Catcher – 'e takes a cut, see. Ev'ry kid they brings in, they gets a fee. Ev'ry barrel of blacking, they makes a profit! An' thanks to Commissioner Bumble, old Barrabas has turned it into big business. Crates an' crates of that stuff are smuggled out ev'ry night under cover of darkness, an' the profits go straight into Barrabas' and Bumble's pockets."

Twill felt a shiver go through her from her grubby golden locks to the hand-me-down boots she wore on her feet. "And no one can stop them?"

"Fagin is a cat with nine lives – a born-again devil!" Dodger's voice was darker than Twill had ever heard it. His eyes were bright with anger, and some other emotion that Twill couldn't quite put her finger on.

"And you're quite sure that it's really Mr Fagin?"

"In the flesh – returned from hell to make London in its likeness," said Dodger, his hands balled into fists at his side. "'E stole my childhood, but I'll be dammed if I let him do that – an' worse – to them boys in there. Not if I can 'elp it."

"Only how can we 'elp it, Dodge?" asked Tommy.

"I 'aven't quite figured that out yet," said Dodger. "But Fagin was once like a father to me, an' 'e taught me to be as cunnin' as he hisself. So I'll think of summat to bring about his ruin. Or die trying!"

Chapter 20

In which Twill forms a plan and the value of
a good education is evident

66**S**umfing oughta be done!" Chelsea declared.
They were back at the printing press now,
where Tommy had been fed and fussed over by the
Sassy Sisterhood and was now being subjected to a bath
– a fate he apparently considered worse torture than
the blacking factory, from the sounds of the screams
he emitted throughout the process, and a procedure
which, it should be noted, had no discernible effect on
the colour of his skin.

"We need to tell Mr Brownlow what's going on,"
said Twill. "Surely he'll put a stop to it."

"Old Brownlow's sick, they say," said Trafalgar, who
worked the patch from Nelson's Column to Big Ben.
"That's what the right honourables up near Downing

Street is sayin'."

"He had one of them strokes, I 'eard," said Fleet, whose expertise lay in robbing the physicians – and their patients – in the vicinity of St Bartholomew's Hospital. "That's the word on the streets near Bart's. Right after young Oliver went away, he got sick. Robbed him of speech and understanding. Won't never recover, the docs say."

"Then Oliver Twist – somebody needs to tell Oliver," said Twill

"That lily-livered boy don't 'ave the gammon to take on old Fagin!" said Dodger with a bitter smile. Since their return from the Benevolent Blacking Factory he had seemed to have a black cloud enveloping him. "You forget that Master Twist an' I wos once acquainted, an' 'e's not made of the same mettle as the likes of you an' me."

"Anyway, he's a kid – wha's he going to do?" said Chelsea.

"He's heir to the Brownlow fortune!" said Twill. "Mr Scapegrace explained that stuff to me, about heirs to fortunes, and power of attorney—"

"Power of what?" demanded Sloane, who worked the Inns of Court and prided herself on her command of legal vocabulary – and her ability to rob judges blind.

124

"It's what happens when an older family member is ill – the heir can get power of attorney and can make decisions about the money and that."

"She's a ripe 'un this one!" said Tommy, who had escaped from his bathing ordeal and was nodding approvingly at Twill.

"But how do you propose that we informs young Oliver of the state of affairs?" Dodger demanded. "He's away, they says – gone to school or overseas or somesuch."

"We write him a letter," said Twill.

The artful young gentleman beheld her with eye-rolling disbelief.

"You can write?" This was little Angel, voicing the general surprise of the congregation.

"I can!" smiled Twill. "An' I can teach you, if you like!"

Angel looked as if she would like that very much, but Dodger was less impressed.

"Beware an educated woman," he said.

"For she shall inherit the earth!" replied Twill.

She grinned and Dodger smiled for the first time that day, though the smile did not quite reach his eyes.

"Come on," she said. "We just need to find out an address to send the letter."

Chapter 21

In which the true sorry and parlous state of dear
old Mr Brownlow is fully uncovered

After Tommy had been subjected to further interrogation and Sloane had been sent to Clerkenwell Green to nab paper, ink and a quill from the stationer's, Twill sat down to write her letter – curiously watched by the entire membership of the Sassy Sisters, plus Tommy. Dodger pretended not to be interested, and was indeed preoccupied by thoughts that seemed to rob him of his usual good humour. But once Twill's work was completed, it was he who insisted on accompanying her through the streets to the residence of Mr Brownlow.

Readers of the tale of Oliver Twist will recall this townhouse of honey-coloured stone on Craven Street as the happy location where Oliver spent a merry and contented time recovering from his arrest, after Dodger had tried (unsuccessfully!) to teach him how to pickpocket, making himself beloved of the man who was to be his future guardian. In those days, the townhouse was well lit, warm and glowing. Peeking through one of the many tall sash windows one might have seen a merry fire burning in the library, or smelled the delectable aromas of roast pork and Yorkshire puddings emitting from the kitchen. But now, as Twill and Dodger approached the house, it was bathed in darkness and smelled only of musty neglect, mildew and misery.

They dared not approach the front door, so they made their way down the area steps and rapped on the kitchen door, which was opened by a thin wraith of a girl – mealy-mouthed, gap-toothed and sour-looking – who surveyed them with the deepest of contempt. "What's your business 'ere?"

"We wondered," said Twill, who had learned from her encounter with the kitchen maid of Doughty Street that deference to the lowest of servants was wise, "might we speak to your master, Mr Brownlow?"

"Master's sick!" declared the mealy-mouthed girl, eyeing Dodger with the greatest of suspicion as if she recognised him from somewhere but couldn't quite recall where. "Can't talk, won't talk. Keeps to his bed all day. Ain't long for this world, Mrs C says!"

"Then Master Oliver, might we speak with him?" enquired Twill.

"Gone away, ain't he?" the mealy-mouthed girl declared with a little gulp. Indeed, she appeared rather upset at the news.

"To school?" Twill asked, hoping that the girl might let slip the direction of the educational establishment.

But she was most surprised by the answer. "Nah – they shipped him off to the Indies, poor wee mite!"

"The Indies?" Dodger and Twill exclaimed in unison.

"Ay, Mr Brownlow 'as estates over there. Sugar plantations – only they's are fallen into trouble. Mr Brownlow won't never use slaves, see – says it's all kinds of wrong – an' tha's been stirring up no end of trouble, cos they still got slavery in them French colonies, see – an' the Frogs get mighty uppity 'bout any Englishman who wants to pay his workers! Somebody needed to go an' sort out the mess and the boy Oliver volunteered, bless 'is kind 'eart." She looked quite teary-eyed as she said this. "Mr Brownlow, he warn't keen on the idea, but dear Master Oliver said as 'e wanted to repay the good old gent's kindness an' do 'is bit to bring an end to the shameful practice of slaving whiles 'e wos 'at it!"

"The Indies!" said Dodger, taking in this momentous piece of information. "Oliver Twist won't survive five minutes out there!"

"That's what Mrs C says too," said the servant girl, who briefly appeared less mealy-mouthed and more sentimental when she spoke of Oliver Twist, causing Twill to suspect that she harboured certain tender sentiments towards him.

"Mrs C?"

"Or Mrs B – I never knows which to call 'er. She's the new housekeeper here. Lady wot looks after Mr Brownlow. Came 'ere shortly after sweet young Oliver left. She sacked all t' other servants. I was the only one she kept on!" The girl pronounced this with a brief flash of pride, but then her face resumed its habitual sullen expression. "She says I need to stop snivvlin' 'bout Oliver Twist. If the climate or the disease don't do for 'im then the French slavers will, she says." At this, the girl gave a giant sniff and looked so melancholy that Twill passed her a handkerchief – the one embroidered with her initials that Baggage had sent her away with – into which the mealy-mouthed girl blew most ferociously.

"So 'ow did this Mrs C – or Mrs B – come to be carin' for Mr Brownlow?" asked Dodger, who had been trying to follow the convoluted train of the girl's narrative.

"She's 'is last link with young Oliver's poor unfortunate mother, God rest her soul," said the girl, whom Twill was beginning to surmise had few people to talk to and could be drawn out quite easily on the topic of her favourite young master. "Mr Brownlow likes to hears Mrs C talk of the girl. An' she makes his medicine – a sort of camomile tea wot 'elps him sleep."

"I bet it does," said Dodger, his suspicious mind working overtime.

"And do you happen to know an address for Oliver Twist in the Indies?" Twill enquired.

"No, ma'am. Only heard Mrs C say something about Martinique – I recalled it because my sister 'ad a sweetheart named Martin an' she thought it such a fine name for an island she reckoned if she'd a' had a little girl they could have call her Martinique."

"A very pretty name, to be sure," said Twill

"Hmmph! Well, 'er Martin's taken up with another girl long since!" said the mealy-mouthed girl, sullen again. "My sister says she'll rip 'er eyes out if she steals her baby name as well as her beau!"

"Thank you so much for your intelligence," said

Twill, sensing that the girl might be about to launch into a further diatribe. "And we hope your master recovers soon."

"Not likely," said the girl with matter-of-factness. "Mrs C says only way Mr Brownlow be leaving this house is in a black box."

Chapter 22

In which things are seen, said and done that
perhaps were better unseen, unsaid and undone

"The Indies!" declared Twill. "How are we supposed to get a letter out to Martinique?"

The pair had turned away from the Brownlow residence and now it was Twill's turn to be disconsolate.

Not so Dodger, who had been pondering on the girl's intelligence and now declared that he had a cunning plan.

"Really?" said Twill. "And does this one involve me having to kiss you?"

"Unluckily for you, Camberwell, it don't!" said Dodger. "An' do you have any better ideas up your sleeve?"

"My name is Twill!" said that young lady indignantly. "And – um – no, I don't."

"Come on then!" said Dodger, before adding cryptically, "cos time and tide don't wait!"

Dodger was unwilling to divulge his plan, so Twill had no choice but to follow as he made his way east across the city. Then they traced the route of the Fleet River, the filthy trickle that runs from Hampstead and Highgate, down Farringdon Lane and Pear Tree Court, Sixpence Lane and Hatton Garden, until it finally meets and joins with the gracious waters of the Thames at Blackfriars.

"Where are we going?" Twill demanded once more.

But to her immense irritation, Dodger was saying nothing. "No time to explain," said he. "And we might be too late already."

Indeed he went at such a pace that Twill struggled to keep up as they passed through the worst slums in the capital where the bright summer sunshine seemed to cast a spotlight on the poverty and desperation therein, as if challenging any passers-by to avert their eyes from the glare. Twill, though she had been some months in the city, could never become accustomed to the sight of an old man, who had sacrificed his limbs fighting Napoleon Bonaparte, begging for a crust of bread; or a clutch of half-naked children — little more than babies

– scavenging in dustbins for food.

They penetrated a maze of close, narrow and muddy streets down by the West India Docks, where the innumerable quays, jetties and warehouses were a hive of activity, even at this early hour of the morning. Twill had not been in this part of the city before, where the air was thick with the rattle of cranes winching cargoes from the ships' holds, the rumbling of empty casks on cobbled streets, and the distinctive aroma of pungent tobacco and the dizzying fumes of rum rising from the holds of ships lately berthed.

"Are you going to explain what we're doing here?" she demanded again.

"All in good time, Camberwell," came the maddening reply.

Dodger told her to stay by a sail-maker's shop while he ducked into various drinking establishments around the docks, all of which seemed to be doing a busy trade, though the sun was still sluggardly rising on the horizon. He was gone over half an hour, leaving Twill perched on a barrel, watching the activities of the mast and oar and block-makers, ship-biscuit bakers, the coal-whippers and pitch-kettles, the sailors and swing-bridge-men around the Limehouse Hole.

Giving up her attempts to figure out what Dodger

was up to, Twill took in her new surroundings with a thrill of excitement and undefined longing. There was a distinctly maritime feel to all the businesses surrounding Shadwell Basin – chandleries with ships' instruments, ropes and hammocks hung in their windows; clothes shops that specialised in "nor'westers" or "sou'westers" (Twill could make out no discernible difference between the two) along with pilot coats, canvas trousers and the coloured shirts beloved of the jolly tar; there were pawnshops filled with a selection of quadrants, chronometers and mariner's compasses; and warehouses brimming with anything from barrels of wine, sherry and rum, to ostrich feathers or furs from Hudson Bay. And the people here were more varied too – this was the one part of London where it was not unusual to hear sailors of all different nationalities talking in a jumble of mother tongues. The whole place filled her with a longing to set sail and see the Seven Wonders of the World.

Just as Twill was beginning to despair of ever seeing him again, Dodger stumbled out of a public house named The One-Eyed Admiral, dragging another young man with him, who was hastily rearranging his collar and tucking his shirt into his breeches, his gait a little unsteady as they approached the jetty where Twill was waiting.

"Where have you been!" she demanded, folding her nose at the smell of rum emanating from her companion. "Are you drunk? And who is this?"

"Twill, meet Harry Bates," said Dodger with a rum-soaked grin that answered her first question. "Brother of me old pal Charlie – now a First Mate in 'Er Majesty's Merchant Fleet."

Twill took in First Mate Bates. He was a handsome young cub with a mess of dark curly hair and a pair of twinkling blue eyes. He in turn looked Twill up and down then flicked a meaningful glance at Dodger, before bowing to our heroine.

"Delighted to meet you, Miss Twill," he declared. "My good friend Jack here never mentioned that he had found so rare and beauteous a lady!"

He delivered this with such a roguish twinkle in his eye that it brought the colour to Twill's cheeks in a most unaccustomed fashion.

"She's no lady!" said Dodger.

"I'm not *his* lady, that's for certain!" Twill responded, just as hotly.

"Well," said Harry with a lopsided grin, "I am disappointed, Dodger. I never knew you to miss out on so rare a jewel."

Again the handsome First Mate shot Twill a smile that made her blush – and Dodger glower.

"But his loss is someone else's gain," continued Harry Bates. "If a fellow might dare to dream…"

Twill's stomach gave a strange little lurch as Harry looked meaningfully into her eyes.

"Can you please stop makin' a fool of yourself an' get to business!" said Dodger, suddenly sober.

"And what exactly is the business?" demanded Twill, hurriedly tearing her gaze from that of Harry Bates.

"Like I says, Harry 'ere works in the Merchant Fleet," said Dodger. "Sailed all over the world, 'e has!"

"You should come with me, Dodge," said the First Mate. "Sign up for Her Majesty's Fleet. You'd have the time of your life!" He slung an arm around Dodger's shoulder, his eyes shining as he described his experiences on the high seas. "You'd not believe what sights, Jack. Trees as tall as the heavens, monkeys with pure golden fur, parrots that can talk in five languages, sea monsters that can swallow a ship whole. I tell you, it's the life, Jack."

As he spoke, Twill's eyes lit up like Chinese lanterns. "It sounds … magical!"

"It is that," said Harry, enjoying the effect his

words had on Twill. "Every day a fresh adventure – discovering new worlds never seen by human eyes, crossing the globe, conquering the high seas."

"Would they take me?" she heard herself ask.

There was a moment's silence. Twill looked hopefully at the First Mate. Then Harry and Dodger both burst into laughter and Twill was brought rudely back down to earth.

"The Navy's no place for the weaker sex, ma'am," said Harry, little realising that his gallantry put paid to any notions that Twill might have entertained on the subject of his twinkling blue eyes. "Fair creatures such as yourself would swoon and fall into the vapours at the sights we daily behold."

"I would not, I assure you!" retorted Twill, tilting her chin and looking so stubborn that Dodger wondered if she might box Harry Bates's ears – and rather hoped she might. "Why, I've a good mind to cut off my hair, swap clothes with Mr 'Artful' Dawkins here, and sign up as a cabin boy! Show Her Majesty's Navy that anything boys can do, girls can do too!"

The image of Twill, hair cropped and in breeches, made Dodger pause, and a strange thought bobbed close to the surface of his consciousness, like a bubble, just out of reach. Then it popped and was gone.

"What about you, Dodger?" asked Harry. "Can we press-gang you into Her Majesty's Service?"

"Can't leave old London," said Dodger with a rueful smile. "Not right now. With the streets so dangerous and so many of my boys in peril in the Benevolent."

Momentarily forgetting her irritation, Twill glanced curiously at her companion. She had not realised that Dodger saw himself as protector of the motherless and fatherless wretches of London's streets. If Mr Bumble had styled himself as Child Catcher in Chief, had Dodger designated himself Chief Child Protector? Was he really resolved not to leave his post till the streets of the capital were safe for the strays and orphans that the state seemed content to leave to starve? The thought recalled her to why they were here. "So do you have a plan or what?" she demanded.

Dodger was already addressing Harry. "You've sailed to the Indies, right? Martinique?"

Bates nodded. "Just back from that part of the world – and sailing back there on the next tide too."

Suddenly Twill saw where this was going and her heart hammered excitedly.

"We're just in time then!" said Dodger. "The Brownlow Plantation. Do you know it?"

"I know it," said Bates. "We docked there last year.

One of the biggest sugar plantations in the whole of the French West Indies, and the only one where slaves ain't never been used – not ever!"

"And might you stop there en route again?" asked Twill, fixing him with an expression so earnest that the First Mate lost himself for a moment.

"Well, as luck would have it, we're due to dock at Martinique to deliver supplies and collect cargo of purest sugar cane. We sail on the next tide on the old sloop *Calliope*."

Twill felt a burst of joy, which lit up her face in a way that was not unnoticed by either of the two young gentlemen present. "Then you can take a letter to the boy Oliver?"

"Oliver?" said First Mate Bates, glancing at Dodger. "Young Twist, is it? I heard plenty about him from me brother Charlie, God rest his soul!" At this, both Harry and Dodger glanced upwards – whether at God or the hovering soul of Charlie Bates was unclear. "Never met him myself though. How old is he now?"

"About 'er age," said Dodger, cocking a thumb in Twill's direction.

"And will I recognise him? How tall is he?"

"About…" Dodger glanced at Twill again, appraising her height. "Yay tall – like that one."

"What of his features?"

"Well 'e looks…" Dodger looked at Twill for a third time, and now his face puckered into a frown. "I suppose 'e has summat of 'er looks about 'im too. Same hair like straw … same bottle-blue eyes too, come to think of it." He wrinkled his forehead into a curious frown. "On'y, Oliver is…"

Dodger looked momentarily rather lost for words, as the bubble of thought that had formed in his brain earlier rose to the surface again. And popped. He gave a curious twitch and dismissed the elusive idea.

"Well, it'll be a fair while afore a message reaches him over there," said Master Harry. "The *Calliope* is as speedy a vessel as you could ask for, but it's a good few weeks' sailing."

"Just get the letter to him," said Dodge. "Quick as you can."

"Anything for a pal of Charles." Harry and Dodger both glanced upwards again, then Harry returned his twinkling gaze to linger on Twill once more. "And for the fair-haired maiden whose image I shall carry with me as a balm over stormy seas!"

Dodger punched him hard in the arm and Twill felt herself flush hotly to the very tips of ears.

So while Twill perched on a barrel to add a few lines to the letter for young Oliver, Harry Bates entertained them with colourful tales of the dangers of the docks. "See that inn over there?" He indicated The One-Eyed Admiral. "That's where the bodies from the coffin ships are brought. There's a back room where they're all laid out – though the official reports will say they were given a sailors' burial at sea – and the medical students from Bart's come and haggle for the parts!"

Twill couldn't help but shudder at the thought as her pen scratched across the sheet of paper.

"And over there..." Master Bates cocked his tricorn hat towards a tumbledown hovel with darkened windows on the corner of Three Colts Street. "The most notorious opium den in all of Europe."

Twill glanced in the direction he was pointing, wondering if Dodger or Harry had ever been inside that particular den of iniquity.

"And just there..." Harry indicated a house just a few doors down from where they were perched, its windows guarded by rusty iron bars that time and dirt had almost eaten away, and with such a look of desolation and neglect about the whole place it made Twill feel as if a shadow had fallen across her heart to look at it. "They say an old apothecary lives there," said Harry. "He'll sell you poisons that will melt your insides, or curdle your blood, or stop your brain so that you are a breathing living corpse."

Twill was unsure whether to give credence to Harry's tall tales any more than to his flirtation and flattery, but as if to prove the young man's veracity, at this very moment the door to the hovel opened and there emerged from within a cloaked figure. A woman, her face fully veiled and her hood pulled low, accompanied by the apothecary – a tiny figure, twisted like an old stick and dressed in faded silken garments that had the appearance of pyjamas. The two were deep in conversation and Twill watched in fascination as the woman handed over a bundle of what looked like bank notes. In return, the apothecary reached into the pocket of his pyjama-garments and handed a tiny green bottle to the cloaked woman.

"What did I tell you!" said Harry, but Twill was straining her ears to hear what the mysterious pair were saying.

"How long?" Twill could just hear the veiled woman say to her companion. "How long will it take?"

"Patience is a virtue," said the old man. "To he who waits good things will come!"

"You said the tisane would stop the old man's brain,

put him completely under our spell," hissed the woman, glancing around like a conspirator.

"And as I promised has it not done?"

Twill turned to look at Dodger, who was listening to the exchange as intently as she.

"Yes, but soon ... soon we need not death in life – but real death, you understand. No more breathing."

Twill felt her heart skip a beat. Could they really be talking about murder?

"Ah – good Mistress Corney! Breath is like the wind," said the apothecary. "When it will blow and wither, who knows."

"No more of your riddles!" A little wind eddied through the docks, swirling away the woman's next words out of hearing, so that Twill caught only the woman's final question: "Will the tincture kill him?"

"Yes – in time, in time."

"Told you," said Harry. "Living corpses – poisonous apothecaries!"

"Shh!" said Dodger and Twill both at once, both straining to hear the woman's next words.

"...but not before the boy returns," she was saying. "We need him alive and under our command till then."

"Only know this do the tides and the fates," said the old man in a thin dry whisper that was barely audible.

The little wind whipped up again, carrying with it the veiled woman's last few words and the hooded figure turned to go. As she did so, the breeze lifting off the sea caught her hood, which slipped just a little, and Twill caught a glimpse of her face – but did not recognise her.

"Corney," Dodger was musing. "Now where 'ave I 'eard that name before?"

Then the sea breeze seemed to shift the tide in both their brains at once and he and Twill turned to each other before declaring in unison: "Mrs C!"

Chapter 23

*In which time passes with no word from
the boy Oliver*

Time passed, as time will. Days rolled into nights
and nights to days. London – that great stage of
human drama – saw its share of entrances and exits,
with little tragedies and comedies enacted daily in the
houses of the great, and in the slum dwellings of
the poor. Fortunes rose and fell, hearts were broken,
babes born, men and women fell in love, married and
breathed their last, and the great wheel that rules the
fates of all – if indeed one believes all human drama
to be scripted by any such higher power – rolled
relentlessly onwards.

First Mate Bates set sail on the good ship *Calliope* and
it is to be supposed he was making his way towards the
Indies, but since nothing was heard of his progress and

the sea can be a cruel mistress, that good sloop might have been caught in the doldrums, or taken captive by pirates, or swallowed whole by one of the giant sea monsters Master Harry claimed to have seen, for all Twill and Dodger knew.

And in the meantime the young pair were busy enough, dividing their time between pilfering from the rich, keeping watch on the Brownlow residence, foiling the Child Catchers and helping small blue boys escape from the Not-so-Benevolent-Boys'-Home-cum-Blacking-Factory. The latter two activities proved to be quite an amusing and vexing sport. For Bumble had employed into his child-catching service men possessed of more brawn than brains, which made tailing them and snatching their quarry out from under their very noses both deliciously easy and incredibly satisfying.

And increasingly necessary – for of late, alarming rumours had started to circulate that the Child Catchers had upped their activities. More and more children were being taken from the streets – and now they were also targeting girls.

A couple of little maidens were said to have been snatched from the Seven Dials; a young female selling posies outside old St Paul's had been taken; and a chop-house girl near The George and Vulture was said to be missing too. The twins, Piccadilly and Trafalgar, claimed to have seen one such girl brought to the Benevolent, but since the tale was told in the secret pidgin-language that only the two of them fully understood, it was hard to be certain. In any case, Chelsea had warned all the Sisters to be more vigilant as they went about their work on the streets.

Sneaking small urchins out of the Benevolent Blacking Factory proved more difficult than it might be supposed, but on this exercise Dodger was hell-bent with a determination that seemed to be borne out of ancient rage. Fagin, however, seemed equally hell-bent on thwarting such efforts. He kept a jealous eye on his illicit enterprise – every door bolted triple, every window barred twice over, every access point cut off. But Dodger was undeterred.

"The old devil ain't giving so much as an inch," complained Dodger. "He don't even take the boys out to church of a Sunday no more. 'E's afraid the good folks of Clerkenwell would spot their peacock-coloured faces an' smell a rat."

There were some successful rescue attempts. They managed to snatch one sky-blue child by grabbing him when he answered the great iron gates to usher in the Child Catchers. Another they pulled up through the small window through which Twill had first spied the activities of the blacking factory. But these odd successes relied heavily on luck and ever-narrowing opportunities.

"We needs to find another way to confound the old devil!" declared Dodger.

It was Tommy Tickle who uncovered a chink in the citadel. For it was he who informed Dodger that each Friday night – long past midnight – a barge made its way up the inky poison of the Fleet river and moored up by the steps behind the house of the Benevolent. A signal from the lantern on board, an answering call from a window above, the grate in the sluice slid open, and the crates of blacking were loaded up on to the barge. This exercise required several boys to handle the cargo, their blue faces lit up like purple pennies in the moonlight, while Mr Fagin watched on, scowling from beneath his red eyebrows.

After Tommy Tickle first divulged details of this weekly enterprise, Dodger and Twill watched from a hidden place beneath a rotting landing stage on the opposite bank, but thereafter they devised a plan. And the next week when the barge appeared, they were ready. While old Fagin was in conference with his supplier, Dodger slipped along the bank and grabbed a blue child.

This small rickety boy – unaware that he was being rescued and more accustomed to beatings than benevolence – struggled like a fish in Dodger's arms and made such a deal of squealing that Dodger had to cover his mouth lest he be heard. Twill held the fortunate child's legs and Dodger his arms, and they managed – not without difficulty – to pull him down to their hiding place beneath the moorings.

"Quiet, ya young wretch!" declared Dodger. "Don't you know youse bein' rescued?"

"Dodger?" The small plummy face looked up at Dodger with astonishment and wonder.

"One an' the same! Now, stay still or you'll have us all into the water," said Dodger firmly, though not unkindly. "An' lord only knows what's in there'll kill us as soon as we take a mouthful!"

The three crouched close to the bank, and a curious rat scuttled up beside them to survey the scene.

Mr Fagin was in earnest conference with the man on the barge, who handed over a bag that seemed to bulge with coins.

"He's rakin' it in!" whispered the Dodger darkly. "Makin' the boys work like dogs, so 'e can hoard like a miserly dragon, sittin' on his piles of gold."

Twill thought she saw more than anger in Dodger's eyes as he beheld Fagin. He had the look of a child abandoned. A look of heartbreak and betrayal.

"I'd like to throttle that miserly old devil and drown him in the Fleet!" Dodger declared.

"Not yet," said Twill, putting a hand on his arm. "Remember what we said?"

"I remember!" said Dodger darkly.

The pair had sat up late at night trying to figure out the tangled web woven by the nefarious players in the Child-Catching-Blacking-Factory-Brownlow game and had come to a pretty fair understanding of the state of affairs – but not yet a complete one. There were certain pieces of the jigsaw puzzle that they had not yet slotted into place, and till they did, they needed to proceed with caution.

"If you blow Fagin's cover now, we won't find out what they're up to next. And then we won't be able to stop them," Twill reminded him. "We need to wait for Oliver."

"But what if 'e don't come?" said Dodger, and Twill saw the haunted look in his eyes that had been there more and more since the reappearance of Fagin. "Or if 'e's worse 'an useless. What then?"

"I don't know," said Twill. "But nobody's gonna listen

to a pair of street urchins. All we can do is keep trying to help boys escape and stop more being captured – and wait."

"Wait for what?"

"I don't know," said Twill. "But something will happen. Something always does."

Chapter 24

In which something happens, as something
always does

Twill was right, of course, and – as things transpired "something" happened sooner rather than later. They managed to get the small blue boy back to the printing press, where a system had been put in place for the cleansing and care of escapees from the Benevolent. The Sassy Sisters set right to work, scrubbing and feeding and fussing over the latest prison breaker, who was greeted joyfully by his former companions. The latest arrival – who had no memory of what his name was, though Tommy Tickle said the boys called him Nemo – was then despatched to the boys' quarters, designated by a sign, imperfectly composed by young Angel, which read "Boys onlee! No gurls".

But just as everyone was celebrating the success of the new rescue method, the door to the printing press slammed open, and Fleet and Sloane entered, looking red-faced and desperate.

"They've taken Angel!" they cried in unison.

"What?" Twill was on her feet immediately.

"Who has? Who's taken her?" This was Dodger.

"Tell us what you saw!" demanded Chelsea.

"We was going down by Greenhill Rents when it happened!" Sloane's one good eye was filled with alarm and she was struggling to catch her breath.

Her panting companion – who looked as if she'd taken a bath in the filthy river that shared her name – picked up the story. "We was hanging round by the Fortune of War pub..."

"Cos the doctors from the hospital drink there, which make it easy pickin's..."

"They don't stand too close to one another cos they stinks, see," said Fleet, who didn't smell too flavoursome herself just then.

"Stinks?" The question came from Tommy Tickle.

"Of death," said Sloane, the scar on her face twitching with anxiety as she spoke. "Them medical students cuts up dead bodies to practise on – so they smells of the grave!"

"Folks keeps their distance – makes it easy to weave in an' out, snatch wot they got in their pockets," Fleet concluded.

"Right – um, I see," said Twill.

"Forget that, what 'appened?" demanded Dodger. "What 'appened to Angel?"

"Well, we was just about to relieve a fancy gent of a very nice pocket watch when the Child Catchers appears!" said Sloane. "It was the big one wot looks like a bulldog, an' that small scrawny one wiv no teeth they calls the Rat."

"We scarpered, a' course – hid in the gatehouse of old St Bart's Church," said Fleet. "But then we sees the little match girl – you know the one wot sells her wares on the corner of Cowcross Street?"

"The one wiv a stump for a leg?" asked Chelsea.

"Tha's 'er," said Sloane. "You remember, we invited 'er to join the Sisterhood back in the spring but she said she'd on'y 'old us back – too slow. Best stick to sellin' 'er matches."

"I remember," said Chelsea, shaking her head with a frown. "We coulda found a place for 'er. Shoulda made 'er come!"

"Well, since then our little Angel always takes 'er a crust of bread when she can spare it," said Sloane.

"An' often when she can't," said Fleet.

"Too kind for her own good, our Angel!" said Chelsea. "Go on – what happens next?"

"Well, the match girl was sittin' there, an' then the Child Catchers swoop down on her."

"So it's true – they *are* after girls now!" exclaimed Battersea, her squashed pug-like face creased in alarm.

"The Bulldog, 'e says: 'We are takin' you under the protection of the City Auf-orities'," said Sloane, in a fair imitation of the larger of the two brutish Child Catchers. "'You 'ave nothin' to fear.'"

"Not likely!" said Dodger.

"An they's talkin' 'bout takin' her to – what did they call it?" Sloane glanced at her companion before adding, "An In-sti-toot for the Edificalation and Betterment of Young Ladies of Ill Fortune."

Dodger and Twill looked at each other. "Never 'eard of it!" says Dodger.

"Doesn't sound good, though," said Twill.

"Sounds worse 'an the Benevolent Home, if you ask me!" added Trafalgar.

"So then what happened?" asked Twill, desperately anxious to learn of Angel's fate.

"Well, the little match girl was crying as piteously as can be," said Sloane, her one eye filling with tears as she recalled the scene. "An' the Bulldog was dragging her by 'er arm, an' the Rat had the other arm, an' nobody done nuffin' to stop it. None of them doctors wot have taken an oath to do no 'arm. Not one!"

"An' afore we knows it, Angel wos over there, beating on the Child Catchers' legs wiv 'er little fists, tellin' them to let go," said Fleet. "She bit the big one, she did, an' 'e gave a yelp like a dog in lime."

"I taught her that move!" said Chelsea proudly.

"Then she kicked the Rat in the shins!" added Sloane. "He howled like the rodent 'e is!"

"Tha's my gal!" said Dodger, like a beaming parent. "Bigger they are, the 'arder they fall – tha's wot I always told 'er!"

"But what happened?" asked Twill.

"So the Bulldog, 'e lets go of the little match girl and turns his truncheon on Angel. An' the Rat, 'e pulls 'er up by the hair, and afore we knows it she's down in the cobbles wiv blood runnin' over 'er face."

"No!" Twill gasped.

"And then they were scooping her up – taking her off, leaving the little match girl crying in the road."

"Ditn't you try to stop 'em?" demanded Dodger.

"A' course we did!" protested Sloane, despair written all over her lopsided face. "We followed 'em, ran hell for leather trying to catch 'em, but there were crowds outside Newgate—"

"There's a hangin' later this morning," added Fleet, equally distressed. "It was like a country fayre down there – folks camped out, hawkers sellin' hot beef rolls and ale, and a fiddler playin'."

"We tried to keep on 'em – tried all we could. Fleet even got a chamber pot emptied on her head for her pains."

They all glanced at Fleet, as the source of her more-than-usually pungent smell became apparent. "But we lost 'em in the crowd," said Fleet, too sorrowful to care about the stink.

"I could still hear her calling!" said Sloane, her one eye awash with briny tears at the recollection. "Callin' out to us, she was, till 'er little voice could be heard no more."

There was silence then for a moment. For Angel was the darling of the Sassy Sisters – a rare water lily bred in a muddy puddle, a child of singular sweetness of temper and kindness of spirit. She brought a sunshine into the dank and gloom of the printing press like a candle in the sanctuary of a holy shrine, and without her the whole place seemed dimmer and darker to all.

It was Twill who finally voiced what all were thinking.

"We have to rescue her," she said. "She can't go to that place – work in that evil cellar till her skin turns blue and she coughs till her lungs burst."

"They don't put the girls in the cellar," said the small boy called Nemo – the one they had rescued that evening, who had barely spoken till now. He was small and bow-legged and hungry-looking, the blue tinge lending his skin an almost ghostly look, as if starvation and ill-use had sent him halfway to his eternal home already.

"What do you mean?"

"They brings the girls to the Benevolent, but then the big lady comes and takes 'em away," he said, looking up at them with frightened eyes (he wasn't yet sure he trusted these girls, who had kidnapped him from the only home he could remember then assaulted him with a bath).

"What? Which lady?"

"Mother Earth, they call 'er," stammered the tiny boy. "She takes care o' the girls, tha's wha' Mr Barrabas says."

"She pays for 'em in gold too," added the boy they had swiped from the gate a few days previously, a red-headed urchin known simply as Ginger. "Mr Barrabas, 'e reckons girls are worth as much as boys nowadays."

"Where does she take 'em?" demanded Dodger, stepping forward so quickly it made the boy flinch. "Wot does this Mother Earth do with the girls?"

"To the in-sti-toot wot she said earlier." Nemo jerked a thumb towards Fleet.

"The Institute for the Edification and Betterment of Young Ladies of Ill Fortune," mused Twill, for none of them had ever heard talk of this place before.

"Tha's the one!" said Ginger.

"An' when does she come? Mother Earth?" asked Dodger. "When does she come to the Benevolent?"

"She always comes on hangin' days!" said the boy called Nobby, who had been dragged feet first through a window by his rescuers and seemed to carry a look of one pulled through a hedge backwards ever since.

"Hangin' days?" Dodger turned to Twill in alarm. "You mean – when there's a hanging at Newgate?"

"Tha's when she comes to collect the girls and take them away," said Ginger the erstwhile gatekeeper.

"But – isn't there a hanging today?" said Twill, looking to Sloane and Fleet, who nodded in confirmation of her fears.

Twill turned to Dodger, who met her glance with an answering nod. "Then we have no time to lose."

Chapter 25

In which Twill turns Twist

"**H**ow are you goin' to get in there?" Dodger asked.

But Twill had already thought of that. Her brain moved faster even than her legs on occasions like this, as her mind darted through the alleyways and passages of the problem and alighted upon a solution several steps ahead of Dodger.

"Pass me some scissors!" she demanded.

"What are you doing?" asked Sloane.

"Dodger – take off your clothes!" continued Twill.

"Tha's very presumptuous, ma'am," said Dodger. "I wonder if we should be better acquainted first."

Twill did not dignify this with an answer. "I just need your breeches! Come on – hand them over."

Battersea produced a giant pair of scissors purloined from a dressmaker in Covent Garden. Twill took them and lifted them to her golden locks.

"What you doin'?" asked Battersea, with a horrified expression on her squashed face that reflected the emotions of the entire company.

"I need to get into the Benevolent Home for Unfortunate Boys. Which means I need to look like a boy in need of benevolence!" declared Twill, brandishing the scissors like a sword.

The others continued to look at her with incomprehension.

"I go dressed as a boy, knock on the gates – say I've been walking for miles, I'm half starved, in need of shelter and food. They'll let me in, I'll find Angel..."

"And then?" said Chelsea.

"Then I'll think of something."

"It's a crazy idea!" said Dodger.

"Have you got a better one?" She held Dodger's gaze and he glowered for a moment. "Exactly," she declared.

Neither did anyone else, so, somewhat reluctantly, the Sassy Sisters set about transforming Twill from girl to boy – borrowing bits of clothing from the former residents of the Brownlow Home, some from Dodger

162

himself (a neckerchief – handed over most unwillingly – but not his breeches to which he held on firmly) and some from an old clothes seller round on Herbal Hill, which had been "borrowed" by Battersea.

The final touch was to cut off Twill's long sheath of corn-gold hair, which was plaited in a coil at the nape of her neck. As she unfurled it and lifted the scissors to cut, everyone in the printing press seemed to hold their breath.

"Stop!" said Dodger.

"What?"

"You can't. Your hair is…" Dodger was staring at her in a kind of confusion. His tongue seemed to tangle his words and his face wouldn't arrange itself quite how he wished it to.

"What?" demanded Twill again.

"It's so pretty," said Sloane, speaking for all of them. "Seems a shame to slice it off."

"Can't you just tuck it into your cap?" said Battersea.

"Not if I'm going to do this properly," said Twill, lifting the scissors again. "An' we can sell it too – bring in a pretty penny!"

"But…" This was Dodger again.

"What?" demanded Twill for the third time.

Dodger shrugged, and shook his head. "Nothing!"

And so – to the mixed horror and fascination of the Sisterhood and the blue boys – Twill's lovely locks fell one by one to the dank ground of Price's Printing Press, and Sloane – who fancied herself in the hairdressing line of work – cut what remained into a neat pageboy style. Dodger had absented himself during this process, apparently to "make enquiries", though nobody was sure into what.

"There," said Sloane, standing back to admire their handiwork.

"We needs to dirty 'er up a bit," said Tommy Tickle, who was perhaps the only member of the company who had enjoyed the spectacle. "She looks a little too fine to be an orphan."

"True enough," said Chelsea, smearing a little soot over Twill's face, in a way that reminded her of Baggage, and almost threatened to melt her resolve.

But it was at this moment that Dodger returned from whatever business had taken him out of the printing press for the past parcel of time. He was hastily stuffing something into his pocket, and when he beheld Twill – now fully attired in her boys' garb – he stopped dead and stared. His expression seemed to undergo several convolutions – from the confusion of earlier, to what seemed a momentary pang of grief, then to amazement, thence to a dawning look of sudden realisation, as if a fact that had been eluding him for some time now suddenly popped into his brain, and all was made clear.

"Of course!" he declared. "I oughta 'ave known it right away."

"Known what?" said Twill, who was becoming a little impatient with Dodger's strange and erratic moods today.

"I knew there was summat – first moment I saw you," he said, apparently ignoring her question and taking a step closer to survey her face with curiosity, as if he were seeing it for the first time. "Where did you say your Baggage found you again?"

"On a rubbish heap," said Twill, who was beginning to think that Dodger might be coming down with some affliction; was he running a temperature?

"Where?" he demanded.

"Um – in a place called Mudfog, I think."

"And the year?" Dodger tipped his head to one side and continued to view her scientifically, like a strange exotic species or specimen in a museum.

"Why do you want to know?"

"Just answer the question, woman!"

"It was the same year they opened the zoological gardens," said Twill, now half convinced that Dodger was under the influence of intoxicating liquor – or perhaps the apothecary's tincture. "That's what Baggage always told me. When I was naughty she said she'd picked up a monkey escaped from the new zoo, not a baby at all!"

"Course she did!" said Dodger, nodding his head, as if all his calculations were adding up in neat columns in his head. "Why, it all makes sense now!"

"What are you talking about?"

But the Artful shook his head. "Nuffin' that needs concern us right now, but p'rhaps…"

"Jack Dawkins, will you stop talking in riddles and let me go and rescue Angel," said Twill, running out of patience. "Before it is too late!"

Chapter 26

*In which Mr Fagin sees a ghost of children past
and Mother Earth reveals herself*

The plan was simple enough. Twill stood before the grey walls of the Brownlow Benevolent Home for Unfortunate Boys and rang the giant bell. A few moments later, the giant iron gates were opened by a ragged-looking child – the replacement for Ginger the Gatekeeper – who looked at Twill in horrified bemusement when she begged to be allowed in, but was too scared to do anything other than usher her inside. As she heard the gates creaking to a close behind her, Twill glanced back at the square, where Dodger and a small team of Sassy Sisters were stationed at watch, and had to swallow down the desire to run back to them. Then she recalled Angel, trapped inside this awful place, and she knew there was no turning back.

"Mr Barrabas is in the workshop," said the urchin with a doleful stare. "I'll take you to 'is office and you can wait for 'im there. 'E's in charge, see!"

So Twill was led through a long room that evidently served as a refectory, with long wooden tables lined with low benches, all covered in filth and grime as if they had not been cleaned for months. Around the room were tapestries depicting the good saviour surrounded by young children, which bore such slogans as "Suffer the little children to come unto me" and "Blessed are the meek". But the place smelled of burned porridge and mould, and there was nothing blessed about it.

Passing through this hall, Twill caught sight of an empty schoolroom, dusty and cobwebbed, which had clearly not been used in some time. Then the urchin opened a heavy door, bearing a sign declaring "No unauthorised entry", and Twill was led down a set of slippery steps, leading down into the bowels of the building.

She could smell the blacking as soon as she began to descend the steps.

"They's smelting a new batch today," said the urchin, a small ship's-biscuit of a waif, known simply as Boy Number Eight. "Always strongest when it's new. Mr Barrabas says it's good for the lungs." As he made this statement, the urchin was wracked with a cough so long and deep, Twill feared it might burst his tiny frame.

And as the sound of the furnace boomed ever closer, Twill felt the noxious vapours creeping into her own throat, ears and eyes. The young boy had led her to a waiting area outside the overseer's office, from which one could view the factory floor below, and Twill could see the small blue boys scuttling like insects, stirring, pouring, sticking, shovelling – all in mechanical unison that seemed so unlike any child that Twill had come across, and so inhuman too, as if their young hearts had been taken out and replaced with cogs and wheels. They barely made a sound to compete with the clamour of the furnace and the bellows and the mechanical thrum of industry – no talk, no laughter, no childish chatter. And their eyes, when Twill fixed on them, seemed glazed – as if the blue of their skin had seeped into their souls, like the colour of sadness.

Twill was so absorbed with this piteous sight that she did not notice that the door had opened and from the factory office had emerged the twisted figure of Mr Barrabas – as the world knew him, or old Fagin to you and me – who stood beholding her with a look of horror on his face.

Now, the reader may recall that old Fagin – when

169

he graced the pages of Master Twist's story – was described as shrivelled, with a villainous and repulsive face obscured by a quantity of matted red hair. In these respects he was unchanged. He no longer wore the filthy old dressing gown, however, but was now attired in an inky black greatcoat, which might once have belonged to an undertaker, along with a large black moth-eaten hat that only half obscured his virulent red eyebrows. His face still held the stamps of villainy upon it – more deeply etched than before and ever so slightly tinged with blue around the eyes – and now, as Twill beheld it, it was contorted into an expression of such shock that it oddly recalled the expression on Dodger's face a few hours since.

"What ... what ... what are you doing here?" he muttered in a trembling voice. "H-h-have ... you come for me at last?"

"What?" asked Twill – with an odd sense of having had this same conversation with Dodger already.

"Tush, tush, my dear! I have eluded justice, slipped the traps of the law – lived like a cat with nine lives ... but have you come to claim me now and take me to my final reckoning?"

"Final reckoning?"

The old man continued to behold Twill with a

horrible expression, as if she were a spirit come from below to unleash its horrors up on him. "Oh, I tremble to hear you say it, my dearest boy. You know I only ever meant the best for you – only the best, dearest boy!"

Twill stared at Fagin in astonishment near equal to that with which he beheld her. His gnarled features were alive with the horror of one who has seen a ghost, as indeed old Fagin believed he had. For before him, shrouded in indigo vapours rising up from the new vat of blacking, stood a young boy so much the image of Oliver Twist that – for perhaps the first time in a life of blackest iniquity – it had stirred up feelings of terror and what even might have been remorse in Fagin's thorny heart, had he been possessed of such an organ in his heartless chest.

He took a step towards Twill, reaching out his crooked fingers. "Is this young Oliver that I see before me?"

"Oliver?"

"Come, let me clutch thee!" said the old man, moving with more agility than might have been expected in a man of his decrepitude, making a sudden dart towards Twill and snatching her hand. She cried out as the old man's yellow fingers came into contact with hers, causing him to jump backwards.

"Warm, I declare. Warm and alive. No ghost come back from the grave to take old Fa— old Barrabas to his fate."

"Ghost?"

Mr Fagin's expression seemed to have undergone several transformations in the space of less than a minute. Now a horrible grin spread across his face, and a new light began to glitter in his black old eyes.

"Oh my dear – could it be?" His tone was milky now – solicitous and smooth. "Are you alive? And returned from the Indies so soon? Saved from the ravages of disease and safely restored to us? Praise be!"

"I'm – I'm not Oliver," said Twill uncertainly.

"Not Oliver, you say?" The old man's expression changed once again. He was regaining some of his composure but still fixed his eyes upon her, wary as a snake preparing to strike.

"Um – no," said Twill, recalling what she had come for – the plan to rescue little Angel – and determined not to be sidetracked by this Oliver business. "My name is Will. Will – um – Camberwell."

"Will?"

"Short for – um – William!"

"It is possible?" said Fagin, creeping towards her again, speaking in a manner that made Twill feel

distinctly ill at ease. "Such an extra-ord-inary likeness…
Tush, tush, my dear! What did you say your name was
again?"

"Will Camberwell," said Twill, concerned that things
were not going exactly according to plan. "And I was
hoping you might give me shelter for the night." She
tried to sound plaintive. "I'm ever so hungry."

"Of course you are, my dear!" said Mr Fagin, his
eyes growing brighter still as he looked over the "boy",
his mind blossoming with possibilities.

"You must stay here, dear heart, and we will look after
you. We will be like family to you. Like the family you
never had." He seemed to twist each word as he spoke,
tugging at the vowels and worrying the consonants in a
most disconcerting manner. "Did you … have a family?
Sisters and … brothers, perhaps? Any … brothers?"

"No, sir," said Twill.

"How remarkable!" said Fagin, rubbing his
gnarled, yellowy-blue palms together as if with eager
anticipation. "Well, well, Mr Camberwell. I am so truly
delighted to see you. Why don't you come with me and
we will make you most at home. We have another new
arrival today and she must be fed and watered before
her long journey too."

As he said this, Mr Fagin, or Mr Barrabas, or the

devil himself – whatever you chose to call him – opened the door to his office and Twill caught sight of Angel, perched on a stool. The little girl looked up and saw her, and was about to cry out but Twill put a finger to her lips and shook her head. Angel looked confused but said nothing.

Twill's mind was moving rapidly, trying to formulate a plan – where was the sluice gate through which the goods were transported? Might she be able to smuggle herself and Angel out without anyone noticing? Could they break through the little window through which Nobby had been pulled? Or make a dash for the entrance like Ginger?

But just then the giant iron doors opened, and all of Twill's best-laid-plans and hopes were dashed, as she heard the words, "My Snow Diamond – fancy finding you here!"

Chapter 27

In which Mother Earth claims her own

She entered like the Queen of the Nile on a burnished barge – gigantic, resplendent, wobblingly white and colossal, rising through the mists of the blue-black smoke on a golden wicker bath chair like a sea monster riding on the waves – or an iceberg rearing its head to wreck the vessel of Twill's hopes.

"Ma-Madam Manzoni…"

"Twill Jones – what a delightful surprise to find you here. Like a diamond in the dust!"

The barge upon which the matriarch of the Black Jack was seated was known as a bath chair – a giant wicker contraption somewhere between a perambulator and a light chaise, typically favoured by elderly gentlemen and the infirm old ladies who visit spa towns to take the water. Mounted on three wheels and named – it was said – because of the similarity of its shape to a bathtub (or, some said, after the watering hole where it had been invented) this particular contraption had been constructed in excessively large proportions. And indeed it needed to be, bearing as it did the gargantuan Madam Manzoni of the Black Jack, who lay like a colossal doll. And propelling this vessel through the burning vapours – with no small degree of effort – were no pretty-dimpled boys but…

"Mrs Spanks!"

"You wicked ungrateful girl!" Spanks panted. "Why, just wait till I have my spoon – and my breath!"

Twill looked from one to the other in horror and confusion. "I … I don't understand. What are you doing here?"

"She's Mother Earth!" stammered Boy Number Eight. "She the one wot takes all the girls."

Twill glanced from the little boy, who was shaking in terror, to the monstrous form of Madam Manzoni who had never, in all of Twill's living memory, left her boudoir in the Black Jack – and yet who now loomed like a vengeful demi-goddess before her.

"Why … why do you call her Mother Earth?" was the only question that managed to surface to her lips.

"Why – because she is the size of a planet!" said Boy Number Eight.

"And because everything that comes from Mother Earth must surely one day return to her," said Madam Manzoni, with a triumphant wobbling purr. "That is the circle of life, my Snow Diamond – don't you know it?" Madam's little piggy eyes flickering dangerously, taking in Twill's boyish garb and severed hair. "That is how I knew I would find you, my dear!"

"You – have been … looking for me?"

"You ditn't fink Madam would just allow you to run off like that?" said Mrs Spanks. "Wiv your debt unpaid – and your monstrous ingratitude burning a hole in her generous heart?"

"I … I didn't think—"

"Of course you didn't!" trilled Manzoni. "And that gave me an advantage in this delicious game of diamond hunting. Meanwhile, my dear old friend Mr Barrabas and his associates in the Child Protection League have been my eyes. I've had them scouring the streets for my little lost girl for weeks."

As she said this, Madam Manzoni turned to Fagin, who had retired to the corner of the room and was surveying the unfolding scene with keen interest, as if weighing up how the new turn of events might be used to his advantage.

A sudden dreadful realisation hit Twill like a short arm jab in the belly. "So that's why the Child Catchers have started taking girls? Because you were looking – for *me*?"

"Mr Barrabas is an old acquaintance of mine," Madam Manzoni continued in gelatinous tones. "Easy enough to commission the Child Catchers to pick up female strays to deliver to my Institute for the Edification and Betterment of Young Ladies of Ill Fortune!"

"But only the pretty ones!" snarled Mrs Spanks.

"Speaking of which – what have we here?" Madam Manzoni's eyes had lighted upon Angel, who had attached herself to Twill's side.

"What a delightful bonus!" exclaimed Manzoni, looking the little girl over as if she were savouring one of Baggage's éclairs. "Eyes like the violet creams to which I am so very partial. Why, she will make quite the Butterfly one day!"

Angel clung tightly to Twill and gave a tiny sob, her big eyes filling with tears – which produced the somewhat unfortunate effect of making her appear only more lovely.

"Leave her alone!" declared Twill. "Take me – take me back, punish me for running off. Do what you want

– but leave Angel alone!"

"My dear Snow Diamond, I do believe you glitter even more brightly when you are angry," said Manzoni. "Of course, it's a shame about your hair, but we can find you one of my old wigs – it might be a quaint, old-fashioned touch. Remind our young gentlemen of their mothers."

Twill was quivering now with a sense of helpless indignation. She was caught in a trap, unable to run or hide, cornered and – what was worse – Angel was trapped with her. And it was all her fault.

"My dear Medora…" Fagin had remained silent but crept forward now, hands held together in an attitude of prayer, his keen eyes ranging hungrily over the scene before him. "Perhaps you might explain something to me…?"

"It's all very simple," said Manzoni, her voice trembling like a lute balanced upon a giant blancmange. "Meet my elusive Snow Diamond – Twill Jones in the flesh."

"So another twist in the tale!" Fagin's eyes lit up dangerously. "Mr Camberwell turns out to be Miss Jones. Why, today is full of surprises, my dear!"

Twill was still madly trying to make sense of the situation. Fagin and Madam Manzoni working in cahoots? But for how long? To what end? Were the Bumbles in on this too? Was this all part of the Brownlow plot? And how was she ever to extricate herself and Angel now?

Fagin took another step towards Twill and reached a gnarled hand out to touch her cheek. She recoiled and Fagin laughed, baring a mouth of brown, decaying teeth in a face as gnarled as a rotten apple. "A pretty little thing and no mistake. I can see why you were so anxious to retrieve her, Medora!"

"I am indeed most indebted to you, Mr Barrabas," said Manzoni, her flesh wobbling ominously. "As she is indebted to me."

"I owe you nothing!" declared Twill defiantly.

"On the contrary. An indenture is a legal document, my girl, and must be repaid!" said Madam Manzoni, as Mrs Spanks produced a scroll, which she unfurled to reveal the papers that Baggage had signed all those years ago when Twill had first come to the Black Jack.

Mr Fagin had snatched the document from Mrs Spanks and was studying it closely. "Well, well," Twill heard him mutter, a sickly smile spreading across his face as he read the fine print of Mr Scapegrace's carefully worded indenture.

"Twill?" said Angel, looking imploringly at the older girl.

"Don't worry," said Twill, pulling her quickly into an embrace. "I won't let them hurt you. I promise."

But her words felt empty. Her brain, which usually dodged and darted through the alleyways of any problem, seemed to have run up against a dead end.

"I'll come back to the Black Jack and pay my debt," she said, realising she was trapped. "I'll work there as long as you wish – if you will only let Angel go."

"Angel – what a delightful name for the little violet-eyed beauty..." quivered Madam Manzoni.

"Will you release her if I come?"

"I don't fink youse in any position to make bargains!" said Mrs Spanks, thin lips pursed. She seemed to be enjoying this as much as she did delivering a good beating with a spoon.

"Perhaps," said Mr Fagin to Manzoni, looking up from the indenture document with a malicious twinkle to his eye, "there is another way that your Miss Twill might repay her debt!"

Chapter 28

*A short episode in which Mr Fagin sees an opportunity
and Twill is caught in a snare of her own making*

The plan was simple – and Fagin had been turning it over in his mind since the moment he had clapped eyes upon Twill, every bit the likeness of her brother.

The indenture document had confirmed a further suspicion in his mind, but this he did not mention to Manzoni – preferring as he did to keep information squirrelled away like jewels, out of sight till he might need it. For now, the resemblance alone was sufficient for his dastardly plan. The rest might become useful later.

"I'm afraid I don't understand you," said Madam Manzoni.

"I wonder if you might consider making a loan

of your Snow Diamond – a small errand, nothing too much," he spoke, with abject humility but with a horrible light in his eyes. "You might see it as a way of repaying the debt to me. And then, my dear Medora, we are even."

"A loan? Even?" The two horrible co-conspirators surveyed each other with undisguised malice.

"I believe there may even be a way, my dear, of making this happy circumstance pay a little more – to our mutual advantage," purred Fagin. "It is – one might say – a golden opportunity!"

"Golden?"

"Nay, Diamond!" said old Fagin, eyes like gaslights in the blue gloom. "Allow me to explain…"

There was a low fire burning in the grate of the office, even though the room was hot and sticky, its walls stained with the sulphurous vapours rising from the factory floor below. The heat and the fumes made it hard to breathe, and hard for Twill to think.

"My dear, she is the very image of the boy, Oliver," Fagin said. "Oliver Twist to the tee. A dead ringer, one might even say! And thus your Twill Jones is the happy solution to the conundrum we find ourselves in."

"Conundrum?" Madam Manzoni eyed him closely.

"Our dear benefactor," said Fagin. "The ever so

benevolent Mr Brownlow, who has proved so amenable of late." He emitted a sinister low laugh and Twill thought of what she had heard of the machinations of the mysterious Mrs C and her camomile tea.

"But his generosity might still be extended further – perhaps to the fullest extent, indeed."

"Indeed!" Madam Manzoni looked most interested.

"And sooner rather than later," Fagin went on. "With a little assistance from young Twill here!"

Twill glared at him angrily. "What exactly do you want me to do?"

Fagin stared back at her. Unbeknown to Twill, he was at this moment recalling the innocent young face of Master Twist – the one child who had eluded him; the one boy who had refused to be moulded into a little criminal like the rest; the one brat who had driven old Fagin almost to the foot of the gallows. This girl had a different look in her eyes – no less pure, but perhaps with more fire. It would be easier to ruin her than her saintly brother, he thought, and, in so doing, he might not only avail himself of a share in the Brownlow fortune, but also stoke the fires of vengeance that he had kept smouldering ever since young Oliver's escape.

"Why, just a little play-acting, my dear. A little haunting. Put a sick man's mind at rest. We will need your Mr Scapegrace to draw up some documents," he said, turning to Manzoni. "The rest should be easy."

"Why should I help you?" demanded Twill, although in truth she already knew the answer.

"Simple, my dear, simple," said Mr Fagin, whose keen eyes had sized up the situation from the moment he understood Twill to be flesh and blood – and female flesh at that. "Because you came here to save the little Angel girl, and so you shall…" He looked at Madam Manzoni significantly. "But only if you do as you are told."

Twill glanced around desperately. She had no choice but to comply.

"Very well, I'll do whatever you ask!" she said. "But only if you let Angel go free!"

"I shall send for Mr Scapegrace to draw up the documents immediately."

Chapter 29

*In which Twill becomes a ghost once more and a
dreadful deception is enacted upon the best and
kindest of men*

And so it was that, as night fell over the city, Twill
found herself in Craven Street in the borough of
Pentonville, outside the residence of Mr Brownlow once
more. Mr Brownlow had, as the reader is aware, been
unwell, his decline in health coinciding remarkably with
the arrival in his household of the new housekeeper,
Mrs C.

There had still been no word from Oliver, and the
rumour was that the boy was dead, lost at sea or fallen
victim to a fever in the Indies, but Mr Brownlow – sick
and debilitated as he was – refused to believe in Oliver's
demise. As did another member of his household – that
same mealy-mouthed kitchen wench who now opened
the door and who still harboured a softness for young

Oliver in her heart, which positively melted anew on beholding his double. She let out a smothered gasp when she saw Twill, still dressed in her boyish garb, her pallor accentuated by the mist that rose up from the nearby Thames and shrouded her in a cloak of white smog.

"Angels be praised!" she cried. "'Tis Master Oliver!" Then the mealy-mouthed maidservant flung her arms around Twill's waist and burst into loud and messy tears.

"Calm yourself, my dear!" said Fagin. "Where is your mistress?"

Her mistress was, in fact, right behind her, and as the mealy-mouthed girl disentangled her snotty face from Twill's breeches, our heroine took in for the first time the lady hitherto known only as Mrs C. She was a plumpish woman; a woman who took great solace in her cats and who had, over the years, come to resemble her favourite feline companion, an overfed tabby who terrorised the mice under the wainscot. She had once perhaps been of the same colouring as that particular puss, but now the curls beneath her matron's cap were peppered with much-lamented grey, and years of scowling had left her once-pretty features with the appearance of an over-wintered pippin.

If Dodger had been present, he would have put things together in an instant. For this was the lady once known as Mrs Corney – now Mrs Bumble by marriage. The good lady of the Mudfog workhouse where Oliver and Twill had been born, who had latterly achieved the dubious good fortune of marriage with the corpulent Chief Child Catcher. Mrs C – Mrs B – Mrs Bumble née Corney: the final piece in the jigsaw puzzle of cruelty and deception practised upon poor Mr Brownlow. Though the details of the plot against Brownlow were still far from clear – even to Twill, who was to play the leading role therein.

"You are welcome, I'm sure, Mr Barrabas," simpered Mrs C, ushering Twill and all the company into the below-stairs kitchen and closing the door quickly behind them. "And this is the girl?" she purred. "Why, you told true when you said she was young Oliver's double."

Behind her appeared her husband – Mr Bumble himself, wheezing and puffing, having been summoned at very short notice by a messenger whose missive had most inconveniently interrupted his dinner of pork chops and ale. He was evidently not best pleased to be called into the house's nether regions, but his expression of consternation changed as he caught sight of Twill.

"Like two sides of a coin, I do declare!" said Mr Bumble, huffing excitedly and looming his giant red face so close to Twill's own that she could smell the port wine and gravy on his breath, mingled with the stench of his rotten teeth, which made her recoil. "A veritable dead ringer, madam! The old man will never tell the difference!"

"This will break his very heart," said a gleeful Mrs Bumble-née-Corney.

"We can but hope," said Fagin, whose malevolence glowed so brightly here in the warmth and comfort of the good man's kitchen that it caused Twill to shiver. "But not before he signs the deed."

"Here," said Mrs Corney with cat-like unctuousness. "Rub a little goose fat on her face to make it glow all the brighter. And let her hold the candle up under her chin – just so – to give a more ghostly impression."

Both were done and the effect pronounced "unearthly" by Mr Bumble, "incredible!" by Fagin, and which provoked an "angels of mercy" from the mealy-mouthed girl, whose name was Anna Dropsy, and who was quite discombobulated by the arrival in her kitchen of Oliver not-Oliver, and a collection of murderous conspirators besides.

"I can't do this!" said Twill, though in truth she still

wasn't sure on the details of what she was doing.

"Consider it an act – if I may say – of charity!" said Mr Bumble, with a tone of impressive pomposity. "You will be helping them paupers as have no work ethic and no purpose in life."

"And helping the old man out of his misery whiles you're at it," miaowed Mrs Corney.

"But I…?"

"No time for buts – we needs to get you changed, then, spit-spot, up you go!"

Thus Twill was shortly ushered up the servants' steps, moving noiselessly across the carpeted hallway, and past a portrait of young Oliver that Mr Brownlow had commissioned and which hung now on the wall. Twill had never – to her knowledge, at least – seen Oliver, and had merely taken the word of those around her regarding her resemblance to Master Twist. If she had given it a moment's consideration, she would have assumed it to be merely a passing resemblance – a trick of the light, an optical illusion in the eyes of the beholder only. But as she stared at Oliver's likeness in oil and canvas, her eye flicked to a mirror that hung on the other side of the hallway and she stopped in her tracks.

Mrs Corney had raided young Oliver's wardrobe

before she sent Twill on her mission, so it was no coincidence that Twill was now dressed in the very same neat blue suit that her brother wore in his portrait. There she stood – dressed identically in every point – and the likeness was more than passing: it ran deep in every contour, in every curve of the mouth, the cut of the chin, the shape of eyes, forehead, nose – the only difference being a greater animation of features on the girl than the boy.

"Why, we might almost be twins!"

Twill had never had siblings, although the ever-changing throng of Butterflies had been like so many older sisters to her, and she had always fancied a brother – someone with whom she might climb trees, play soldiers, make mud pies, race with the hoop and ball, collect insects, and plan raids on the neighbouring gangs. Someone with whom she could exchange dares and dreams, who might join her on the adventures she embarked on in her head every day and dreamed of before she fell asleep every night. Looking at Oliver's likeness was like looking at the brother she had never had, and though she fancied he might not perhaps have been the mud pie and insect type, she felt equally sure she would have liked him. Nay, she felt certain they would have been the very best of friends. And the thought made her feel both happy and suddenly indescribably sad.

The girl – Anna Dropsy – stood behind her bearing a candle, and was also staring from one picture to the other, her mouth open in wonderment and confusion.

But Mrs Corney had no time for mirror-gazing. With a "Stop dawdling, an' get in there!" she snatched the candle from Miss Dropsy and gave Twill an almighty shove through the door and into Mr Brownlow's bedchamber.

The old man lay in a giant old four-poster bed, a shrivelled figure and a mere shell of the kind and elegant gentleman he once had been. The bed itself looked as if it had not been changed for weeks, and the room was in a similar state of disarray. Dust collected on the dressing table whereon a hotch-potch collection of potion bottles, tea cups and crumpled pieces of paper lay. The floor was scattered with the debris of the sickroom and over all hung a bitter stench of sweat and sickness and something else that was oddly familiar, though Twill could not say why.

A shaft of moonlight fell through the window on to a patch of carpet directly before the bed where Twill stood. And thus it was that when old Mr Brownlow opened his eyes, he saw her glowing. The very face, the very figure that he had seen in his fevered dreams, that he had conjured in his ailing imagination, envisaged in his prayers, now stood in a shaft of moonlight before him – like a long-hoped-for and long-given-up-on miracle.

"Ol-i-ver!" he managed to whisper through parched lips. "Is … that – you?"

Twill swallowed hard. Doing this to the good old man felt so cruel, for his face had lit up on sight of her with such hope that she felt loath to continue with the deception.

"Yes, my dear guardian," she stammered. "It is!"

"Oh, my boy – I knew you would come!"

"I came, sir."

She glanced towards the door, which stood ajar and behind which she knew Mrs Corney was watching her every move. She knew what they had told her to do – but surely she might give the man some peace and a moment's brief happiness before she crushed it forever?

"Come here, my boy. Let me look at you," whispered the good old man.

Twill took a step towards the bed, careful to stay in the path of the transformative moonlight, as she had been told.

"Closer, my boy."

She took another step towards the bed and she could see now that the eyes of Mr Brownlow were glistening with tears. The old man was much transformed since the departure of Oliver. His decline in health had been rapid – hastened by the arrival of Mrs Corney, with her tinctures and restorative teas, which had muddled rather than restored his mental faculties. His skin was now papery white, his eyes sunken into dark sockets and he looked as if he had not eaten properly for weeks. Twill longed to reach and take his claw-like hand, or dab a cloth over his parched lips but she knew she must not touch him for fear of breaking the illusion she was supposed to be creating.

"Why, you look so like your mother," said Mr Brownlow with the saddest of smiles. "You grow more like dear Agnes every day."

At this, the old man waved his hand towards the other side of the room, where Twill saw another portrait on the wall. Her eyes met with those of the girl it portrayed – and she gasped.

Twill had barely taken in the shock of seeing her own face in that of Oliver Twist. She had not had time to consider the significance of the resemblance, yet it had left her with an undefined sense of longing. And now, as she stared at this second portrait, glowing in the moonlight, she felt the fire of that longing blaze up once more. For there before her she saw another image of herself. Not the hair-shorn urchin she was now, nor the kitchen girl at the Black Jack. This image recalled that brief moment when she had been transformed into the Snow Diamond – when she had worn a silken gown with her golden hair piled on to her head and little paste diamonds hung from her ears. She had seen her own reflection then in the Butterfly boudoir – and now she saw the same face in the portrait on the wall.

But she saw something else too. Something in those soft blue eyes and the gentle curve of the lips that she could not quite put her finger on – as if she beheld the ghost of a long-lost beloved; someone she had never known yet had spent her whole life missing. It made her feel as if the ground had shifted under her feet, as if the moonlight had remoulded the whole world and opened up her eyes to shadows and strange shapes that she could not yet understand.

She turned from the picture, feeling dazed. Mr Brownlow was reaching a skeletal hand out towards her. "Come, let me touch you!" said that good old man. "Let me believe you are real! I have dreamed so long of this moment. They told me you had died…"

"Guardian…" Twill started to say.

"But I knew it could not be true. I knew you must still be alive."

"Mr Brownlow – sir, I…"

Twill glanced towards the doorway where Mrs Bumble was making a series of angry gestures.

"Come, my dear boy!" pleaded Mr Brownlow. "Let me take your hand and feel that you are real."

Twill took a step forward. She longed to give him the consolation he begged for, and she was filled with an indefinable desire to make contact with this good old man, whose eyes beheld her with such love – but she had her instructions.

"Guardian, I—"

But she had no chance to say more, for at that moment the door opened and Mrs Corney entered, declaring loudly, "Why, Mr Brownlow, what are you doing disturbing yourself? Lie down and rest. I've bought you more of my delicious camomile tea."

Chapter 30

In which deeds are done, and deeds are signed, which will be of much import later in the tale

Mr Bumble's wife was carrying a steaming tincture from which emitted an odour that was definitely *not* camomile. It was the same smell that lingered in the room – the same that Twill had encountered somewhere before, though she could not recall where: a vile, noxious aroma that made her head swim and her stomach turn.

"Look! Look, Mrs Corney!" said dear Mr Brownlow, his eyes bright as a child's on Christmas morning. "Oliver has returned. Oliver is back!"

Mrs Corney turned in mock surprise, surveyed the room, stared right at Twill, and then straight through her. "Where, Mr Brownlow?" she said with exaggerated incredulity.

"Why, there, Mrs Corney, right there. My Oliver is back – don't you see him?"

"Why, I see nothing," said that wicked woman, apparently unconcerned with breaking a noble heart.

"But he stands there – he lives, he breathes. He spoke to me." The old man's voice was little more than an impassioned whisper.

"Oh, dear, dear Mr Brownlow," said Mrs Corney, the very picture of disingenuous concern. "I fear it is the fever of your brain playing tricks on you. Young Oliver is dead – do you not remember? We had a letter. Poor lad – he died of the sweats out in Martinique."

"But – I can see him!" the old man insisted, eyes boring into Twill so hard she felt as if they might tear a hole right through her. "He is looking right at me."

"My dear sir, there is nobody in the room but you and me, unless … perhaps!" Mrs Corney put a hand to her mouth and widened her eyes so far that Twill wondered if the woman might have considered a career on the stage.

"Perhaps…?" whispered Mr Brownlow.

"Perhaps he is a ghost, come to call on you from the dead," suggested Mrs Corney. "Or to give you a … message?"

She turned to Twill then and fixed her with a

meaningful gaze.

"A message…" whispered Mr Brownlow, staring at Twill as if she were an apparition that might disappear if he allowed himself to blink.

"Yes, yes. Now I come to think of it, I expect young Oliver's ghost *has* come to tell you something…" Mrs Corney stared pointedly at Twill again. "Perhaps about your will?"

"My will?"

"I—" Twill started to say.

"He spoke!" Mr Brownlow's face was reanimated: Twill's single syllable seemed to breathe new life into him. "Did you not hear him?"

"I heard nothing," Mrs Corney said with an impassive expression that made Twill want to strike her. "What is he saying to you?"

"Speak again! Speak again, my boy, I beg you."

Both occupants of the room were staring at Twill intently, willing her to say more. She opened her mouth to speak … but no words came out.

"Why, I do believe an angel sent him – an *angel*," Mrs Corney said, with an exaggerated emphasis designed to remind Twill of the little girl still in Madam Manzoni's clutches.

"Oh, my dear boy," whispered Mr Brownlow with

such an imploring look in his eyes that it nearly broke Twill's heart. "How I long to hear your voice one last time."

"I am so sorry…" muttered Twill.

"Oh," said Mr Brownlow, his face lit up with joy. "What can you have to be sorry for, dearest of boys?"

"My beloved guardian, I am so sorry," said Twill, tears in her eyes now. She tried hard to recall the words that Fagin had made her rehearse – tried to say them now, though each seemed to stab at her heart as a betrayal. "Now I am in the grave … past all help … I beseech you to bestow your fortune…" Her voice cracked and she could not continue.

"Go on, my boy. I will do whatever you ask!"

It was the cruellest of deceptions practised on the best of men – and yet Angel's safety depended on it.

"To bestow your fortune…" she stammered as Mrs C stared at her with glistening joy, "…to help other … destitute urchins … as I was once."

"Why, I believe he wants you to alter your will," said Mrs Corney, suddenly forgetting the pretence of not being able to see or hear the "ghost".

"My will?" whispered Mr Brownlow, so transfixed by Twill that he was unaware of the inconsistency. "My fortune?"

"Yes – yes," said Twill, desperate suddenly to get this over and done with. "You must change it. Leave all your fortune … leave it all to the Benevolent Home boys…"

"And the girls' institute too," added Mrs Corney.

"And the girls too," added Twill perfunctorily, her voice breaking on the final word so that it came out as little more than a sob. She was suddenly exhausted, wrung out by the waves of emotion that had washed over her in the past few hours, her mind clouded and confused as she held Mr Brownlow's gaze and felt the force of his love blazing so strongly upon her. The only person who had ever looked at her thus was Baggage, and it made her long for that good woman's warm embrace – a longing so powerful she felt as if she could barely breathe.

"Of course, my dearest boy – I shall do as you ask," Mr Brownlow whispered hoarsely, his eyes clouded with tears. "For the suffering you and your dear mother had to endure I will make this bequest so that others do not have to. You may rest in peace, my boy."

"Thank you. Thank you, my dear, beloved guardian," Twill managed to whisper, hoping her final words might bring some comfort to mitigate the cruelty she had practised upon him.

"Mrs Corney, fetch me a lawyer," said Mr Brownlow.

"Why, yes, sir. Right away, sir," said Mrs Corney. Then she glanced at Twill, who remained unmoving. "I expect the spirit will go now that it has imparted the message." She jerked her head towards the exit.

But Twill could not bring herself to leave the old man so desolate. She took a step forward and, before Mrs Corney could stop her, she took his withered hand in hers, bent low and planted a kiss on his papery old forehead.

Mrs Corney let out a gasp and leapt forward to grab her, but not before Twill had managed to whisper a single command in Mr Brownlow's ear: "Don't drink the tea!"

Chapter 31

*In which old friends return and some prove more
friendly than others*

There was one last ghastly surprise for Twill. She stumbled back out on to the landing, past her brother's portrait and down the back steps to the servants' kitchen – barely able to see through the tears that clouded her eyes. And there, standing by a fire that roared far more merrily than that in Mr Brownlow's room, before a table set with food and drink far more inviting than the master of the house enjoyed, was Mr Scapegrace.

Twill, reeling from the events of the evening, started towards her old friend with joy. The dusty little man, who had not left the Black Jack for over half a century, was the first friendly face she had seen in what felt like days (though it was, in truth, merely a matter of hours since she had departed the printing press). Yet to her surprise, his face looked anything but friendly and he did not meet her eye.

"I'll take the documents up at once," he said, in flat dusty tones, blinking like a mole come up unexpectedly into the light.

"But, Mr Scapegrace…"

Her dear friend and tutor met her imploring gaze without seeming to see her. He appeared smaller here, out of his study – his shoulders stooping, tiny grey eyes behind half-moon spectacles not meeting hers. It was as if he no longer recalled the happy hours they had spent poring over tales of Arabian Nights, puzzling through Pythagoras and conjugating Latin like a pair of cackling geese: "Hic, Haec, Hoc!" But that was the Mr Scapegrace of the Black Jack. And it seemed that outside that establishment he was a completely different person altogether.

"If you'll excuse me," he said, shuffling past her.

Twill moved aside with a shock of sadness. The evening had turned so many certainties on their heads, presented her with impossible choices and confusing new revelations – and now here was another shocking blow. She felt confused, disorientated, sick with disappointment and shame – but most all fear, a terrible fear that her actions had made things not better but instead far, far worse for all concerned.

Twill was barely aware of the journey back to the Benevolent Home. Mr Fagin – despite his recent transformation into the role of Mr Barrabas – did not like to be seen out on the streets of the capital. So they made their way back on a barge along the Thames to Blackfriars, then up the filthy tributary of the stinking Fleet. Twill was not aware of the stench of the effluvia; she did not see the looming buildings, the tanning factories and slaughterhouses and slums that lined the tarry sewer; she was barely aware of the flicker of the barge lamps illuminating the smog-smothered water, nor the distant dome of St Paul's rising like the fretted roof of heaven beneath the starry skies. She could only see in her mind's eye Mr Brownlow's face staring at her, and recall the desperation in his voice as he implored her to speak. She could only think of how she had handed all the power into the hands of her enemies and placed the old man in deadly peril. For once Mr Brownlow signed away his fortune what would become of him? Once the conspirators had bled him dry and had no more use of him – what then? She had been in the old man's company less than half an hour, yet his fate weighed heavily on her heart.

She was still consumed with these thoughts as they reached the sluice-gate entrance to the Benevolent Home, and so it was that Twill did not see the figures crouching in the shadows along the banks as they approached, nor notice the high-pitched whistle – as of a country bird – that went up from under a crumbling footbridge as they alighted from the barge. Mr Fagin seemed also unaware of these circumstances; perhaps he was dreaming of Mr Brownlow's fortune as he hurried his young charge towards the sluice. Whatever the circumstance, he and Twill were both taken by surprise by the ambush that ensued.

For as the sluice gate rose, a loud cry went up and then a series of answering calls, and the party on the barge were overwhelmed by an onslaught of dark figures who charged towards them.

"The boys – get the boys!" a voice shouted – a familiar voice.

"My Twill!" shouted another – more familiar still. Baggage? Here?

"Get the old devil!" This in the unmistakable tones of Dodger.

In the confusion, Twill could barely see what was happening, for the bandits seemed to pour into the sluice gate while she herself was pulled roughly backwards, her arm scraping hard against slimy brickwork, her feet lifted bodily off the ground. Mr Fagin had been apprehended as he tried to scramble up on to the wharf by Old Seacoal Lane and Twill could see, by the light of the barge lamp, that Dodger had him by the throat.

"You old devil – you old devil!" he was shouting. "I should finish off wot they should 'ave done at Newgate!"

The old man's face was yellow and weasel-ish in the gaslight. "Come now, Dodger!" he said with an evil leer. "I was a father to you, my dear!"

"You were!" Dodger cried, and in the heaving light cast by a swinging lantern Twill could see that his face was contorted, his eyes shining with moisture. "You were!"

And then Twill was being dragged backwards into a narrow tunnel and there were small figures everywhere small figures that, even in the gloaming, she could see were clearly blue. Boys – blue Benevolent boys – pouring out of the sluice gate like rats, lead by a Pied Piper figure who looked a lot like Chelsea, aided by the Saffron Hill Sisters, who carried, tugged or shoved the blue boys out on to the wharf and sent them scattering off down tunnels and alleyways in all different directions.

And could that be the Bob the butcher's boy – with two blue urchins held neatly, one under each arm like sacks of flower – heading for the footbridge that led to Saffron Hill?

And Baggage – could it really be Baggage who was pulling Twill tight to her bosom and sobbing, "Oh, my Twill – my Twill. I thought I'd lost you forever!"?

Chapter 32

*In which the back room behind the pump at the
Three Cripples becomes headquarters for the
counter-attack*

"Baggage? What are you doing here?"

"Rescuin' you, tha's what we'se doin'!"
A beaming smile lit up Baggage's crumpled features,
making it more beautiful than any face Twill had ever
seen.

"But how did you even know…?"

"The coachman wot they sent for Mr Scapegrace –
'e tipped Bob off," said Baggage. "He knows everyone,
does my Bob. Finger in ev'ry pie – as they says."

"Oh, Baggage," said Twill, her heart so full she
thought it might actually burst. "You don't know how
I've missed you!"

"Don't I such?" said Baggage reprovingly. "When
not a day's gone by I haven't cried myself to sleep for

aching for my little Twill! I told Bob I woultn't rest till I found you again, an' now here you are!" She flung her arms around Twill's neck, and all that Twill longed to do was pour all of the day's woes and worries into her warm bosom.

But Baggage pulled away quickly, businesslike now. "But there's no time to be gettin' silly – we needs to get you away. Once Madam knows youse gone there's no telling what she'll do."

"Madam…" Twill recalled with a start. "Angel – she has Angel!"

"Don't you fret. The Sisters be rescuin' the little Angel," said Baggage. "I wos to get you, Bob's helpin' with the boys and the young man the girls call Dodger was dealin' with the wicked old man. We're all to meet back at the Cripples."

The old printing press had been deemed too dangerous to return to for fear its location might have been compromised, so it was decided that the raiders of the Benevolent would reconvene back at the public house known as the Three Cripples, where a chamber behind the pump room, hidden from view by a false wall, was to be the headquarters of the counter-attack conspiracy.

Twill and Baggage made their way through the

slums of Hatton Garden, into the area they called the Rookery. In daytime this slum was home to the traders who purchased "secondhand" (ahem!) silk handkerchiefs and pocket watches from the pickpockets, and these gaudy flags could be seen everywhere, dangling from pegs outside windows or flaunting from doorposts. At early morn and at the setting in of dusk, this emporium of petty larceny was visited by the silent merchants or "fences" who traffic with stolen goods in dark back parlours and go as strangely as they come. But by night the place was more sinister still – strange figures hung in the shadows, the skeletons of crumbling buildings loomed like flayed corpses and strange noises permeated the air – thuds and screams rising up from within the hovels and dank cellars as if the whole area was populated by poltergeists.

Twill was used to this by now, and Baggage was too fired up with rescuing zeal to be disconcerted as they hurried towards the notorious drinking den known as the Three Cripples – an establishment as dilapidated as its name appeared to suggest, but from which came the sound of raucous laughter, the out-of-tune twang of a piano being played with extraordinary gusto, and a cacophony of voices raised in song, with just one sweet note soaring high above the rest.

As they pushed open the door to the public house, the sound swelled and Twill saw an old man at the piano who looked no younger than one hundred and fifty years old. He had but one leg and one eye – when the general prejudice runs in favour of two – but this did not stop him from banging on the pedals of the old pianola as he belted out the notes of the song.

And next to him stood a girl who delivered the single sweet chord that ran below the rousing chorus of the rest. The singer – whose name was Bet, and who readers may recall as the erstwhile friend of one Nancy (heroine of the tale of Oliver Twist) – sang of lost friends and a love worth dying for, sentiments that lent such sweet melancholy to her voice that one might have guessed that she too recalled that good fallen woman who had given everything to protect young Oliver.

But now was no time for sentiment. Baggage caught the eye of the publican – the same stout and pragmatic gentleman who had been custodian of the establishment since the days of the villainous Mr William Sikes – and he rose discreetly, indicating that the girls should follow. He led them past the snug and into a corridor that appeared to house only a shelf of barrels but, with a gentle tap in the right spot, revolved creakily to reveal an aperture – a door into a secret room behind the wall.

What purpose the publican had for such a room may only be surmised, but if the government will place exorbitant taxes upon the importing of liquor then perhaps they should not be surprised if barrels of such stuff find their way into the country by other means – and such contraband must be stored somewhere! For today, however, the room was to serve as hiding place for smuggled boys, some of whom were already secreted away in there.

"Lawks a-mercy – why are they blue?" demanded Baggage.

"Long story!" said Chelsea, who had returned just before Twill and Baggage.

"'Tis the old devil's black soul staining the very air!" said a voice from the doorway. Dodger – returned from the fray – was looking very much the worse for wear. His jacket was torn and bloodstained, his nose plastered in the same red gore, and his beloved top hat nowhere to be seen. But worse than his appearance was the expression on his face. He looked crushed, broken, unmendable.

"What is it?" asked Twill, rushing over to him. "Dodger, what happened?"

"Why, 'e's like a very serpent! One minute I 'ave him

in my grasp, then he some'ow slips away an'..." He looked at Twill desperately. "Angel!"

Twill's heart lurched in her chest. "What of Angel?"

"I 'ad him right under the sluice gate," said the Artful, each word paining him to tell. "Woultn't 'ave minded if it 'ad fallen on his neck like a guillotine – cut that scrawny devil's throat once an' for all. But the fat lady had Angel and she was screaming and I ... I let him go – I had to – to save her." He looked at Twill in desperation. "Only I was too slow – an' now they've got 'er still."

"So it was all for nothing!"

"Not for nothing – no! Look at all the boys we set free!" said Bob the butcher's boy, who had just appeared through the secret doorway with a basket of rolls and currant buns, which he began distributing to the hungry escapees.

"An' you too, my Twill," said Baggage, her dear old face filled with love, and unable to take her eyes off her darling. "Oh, you are a sight to make the 'eart sing. An' I do declare you is even more beautiful than you wos – even dressed as a boy – ain't she?"

Here she turned to Bob and Dodger as the two male arbiters of beauty in the room. Bob looked awkward and muttered something about "beauty and beholders

… an' some prefers a more comfortable face…" while Dodger's cheeks coloured to the shade of his bloody nose as he declared that he'd "never given the matter much thought – too busy for wenches and women and … and…" before changing the subject altogether and declaring loudly, "We needs to stop 'em!"

"Yes!" said Twill. "We have to save Angel – and poor dear Mr Brownlow too! For I fear he is in mortal danger. But how ever it is to be done?"

"Don't you fret!" came a voice from behind, and they all turned to see an unexpected figure standing in the doorway, who declared, "Mr Scapegrace is on the case!"

There was a stunned silence as the assembled company stared at this most unlikely of visitors: young Miss Anna Dropsy.

"He told me to bring you this!" said Dropsy, no longer looking mealy-mouthed but proudly heroic, as she withdrew from her cloak a piece of parchment, which she handed to Twill.

"But – I don't understand. I saw him at Mr Brownlow's."

Twill was still trying to make sense of events that were moving at dizzying speed. "He seemed so…" She recalled the cold-eyed stare of her erstwhile tutor

215

with a shudder.

"Well, 'e couldn't rightly let Madam suspect he wos on our side, no!" said Baggage. "An' the dear old man's been in love wiv the mistress since she wos a Butterfly."

"Madam Manzoni was a Butterfly?" Twill and Dodger both exclaimed in unison.

"But 'e loves you wiv a father's love," said Bob.

"An' a parent's devotion is strongest in the world!" declared Baggage.

"Madam's mistake wos to fink his loyalty to 'er would be stronger than any other attachment," said Bob, for it seemed the Black Jack gang were all in on this latest plot turn. "But 'e would do anything to save you, young Twill – anything."

Twill was still confused.

"Them documents wot he drafted for Mr Brownlow to sign," Anna Dropsy went on, "Mr Scapegrace crafted the wording so clever – an' your Madam trusts 'im so deep she don't bother to check."

"Check what exactly?"

"Before Brownlow signed 'is fortune over to them rascals, 'e signed over power of attorney to his ward," said Baggage cheerfully.

"Dear little Oliver Twist!" Anna Dropsy beamed at Twill.

"I see!" said Twill, though she wasn't sure she did. "But – um – what does that actually mean?"

"And what do we do now?" demanded Dodger.

"Well, the lawyery old fella – your Mr Scapegrace – 'e says they'll be goin' to the Farthingale and Shillingsworth Bank tomorrow," explained Anna Dropsy, screwing up her face as she recited the instructions she had carefully memorised. "To withdraw the funds, 'e says."

"So soon!" exclaimed Twill.

"An' only Oliver can stop 'em," added Anna.

With dawning comprehension, Twill saw the plan her tutor had in mind – a plan to save Mr Brownlow and keep Oliver's inheritance from the hands of the villains – and it was nothing short of brilliant. Recalling the blinking gaze of Mr Scapegrace she made a mental note to commend him later on his superb acting skills.

But then something occurred to her.

"What about Angel?"

"Tha's the bit we needs to figure out!" said Dodger.

"Leave that to us!" said Chelsea. "She's one of the Sassy Sisters. We will bring our girl home!"

That night was an uneasy one. Desperately tired as Twill was, there was so much playing on her mind that she could never have slept were it not for Baggage, whose warm comforting presence acted on her like a sleeping draught. For a long time they sat side by side, propped up against barrels of contraband rum and surrounded by the slumbering figures of blue boys and Sassy Sisters. Bob had fallen asleep with his mouth open and was emitting a series of low snorting noises, whilst Dodger slept bolt upright with what looked like one eye open, his head twitching every now and then as if he were still fighting old Fagin in his sleep.

"I'm sorry I didn't live up to your high hopes of me!" whispered Twill, her eyelids drooping as the soft wings of sleep crept across her brow. "You wanted me to be a ladies' maid and here I am – a lawbreaker and a fraud."

"An' I couldn't be prouder!" Baggage replied – the last words Twill heard before she finally drifted off to sleep.

Chapter 33

In which the tale Twists and Turns

The next morning the counter-conspirators dined on bacon and eggs provided by the publican of the Three Cripples – who himself bore an ancient grudge against Mr Fagin for the role the villain had played in the downfall of Miss Nancy. Then they went over the plan once again – Twill struggling to get her head around the codicils and caveats and chattels and culpas and contingencies of Mr Scapegrace's documentation. She wasn't at all sure she understood the legal niceties of the plan – nor was she convinced that the plot would work at all – but it was the only chance they had. She had to try.

So Twill was got up once more in her "Oliver togs" as the Sassy Sisters had taken to calling them, whereupon

Mr Jack Dawkins told her she looked "regular daft in that get-up", and yet was for some reason unable to look her directly in the eye. Then she and Dodger made their way down the Strand to Trafalgar Square, to the headquarters of Farthingale and Shillingsworth Bank. The sun was shining as they stood before the imposing building – a regular wedding cake confection in white Bath stone, adorned with a plasterwork frieze that appeared to depict two merchants standing before a young judge holding a pair of weighing scales in one a hand and a knife in the other.

"I wonder what story it's supposed to represent," thought Twill, making a mental note to ask Mr Scapegrace when all this was over. *"If the plans works!"* she added silently to herself.

For if the plan did not work, she too might find herself facing a judge before nightfall – and locked up in Newgate by morning! For was she not impersonating a very well-known young man who was heir to a very large fortune? And had she not duped a very well-known philanthropist and benefactor to the city? And had she not persuaded that well-known old man to sign over power of attorney under false pretences? If she was found out, the law was not likely to look kindly on her – or any of her party. For what judge would find in favour of the vagabond imposters over the respected beadle and his cohort?

"You can do this!" Dodger had appeared by her side as Twill stood, staring up at the giant marble portico.

She turned and beheld Dodger, who managed to meet her eye for the first time in nearly two days. "What if I can't?"

"A' course you can! First moment I met you, I says to meself – there's a regular rum 'un – a girl wot can keep pace with the Dodger!"

"I can *outpace* you, actually!"

"If you says so!" Dodger shrugged. "But it's not often I comes across a girl wot can match me. Not since – well, not since dear old Nancy." His face softened as he spoke. "You reminds me of 'er, as it 'appens – same lion heart and stubbornness. She was the only one wot could ever outsmart old Fagin – and not cos she was faster or cleverer but cos she cared more an' anyone else 'bout what was right and wrong. And that's you, right enough."

Twill was momentarily lost for words. She was accustomed to Dodger's insults but this serious Dodger who spoke softly – well, he rather bamboozled her.

So it was with this dubious encouragement that Twill made her way up the white stone steps, pushed open the heavy mahogany door and found herself in a high-ceilinged vestibule with austere oak panelling and marble fretwork that stretched up to a domed roof on which carved cherubs frolicked. On the walls loomed portraits of severe-looking men – ancient Shillingsworths and Farthingales stretching back many generations, some bewigged, some bearded, some powdered but all sharing the same grim expression, frowning down upon those with the temerity to cross the marble chessboard floor into the hallowed halls of the bank.

A light porter stood at the doorway, nose raised in the air, a disdainful expression on his face.

"I am here," Twill informed him, her chin up and her shoulders back so as not to betray her nerves, "to meet with the managers, Messrs Farthingale and Shillingsworth."

"I'm afraid they are engaged with other clients and cannot be disturbed," said the porter, who was a very light porter indeed, having hair so pale it was almost white, and eyelashes so luminescent his milky grey eyes looked bare and unfringed.

"Trust me," said Twill. "My business is of such import that they will not object to the intrusion."

"Indeed?" snuffled the porter, eyeing her with a

mixture of suspicion and deference.

"My name," she declared, fingers crossed behind her back, "is Oliver Twist!"

This seemed to have an effect on the light porter, who sniffed loudly and then, speaking through his nose as if he was suffering from a heavy cold, conceded. "I shall enquire. Come with me."

Led by this young man, Twill made her way past rows of stooping grey bank clerks, sitting at desks writing in large leather-bound ledgers. Though she was trembling inside, she tried to carry herself as she supposed a young man of means might do in such a setting, holding her head high, and pulling her shoulders back. But when through the glass windows of the office of Messrs Farthingale and Shillingsworth Twill saw that the clients with whom they were conducting business were none other than Bumble and Barrabas and the formidable Madam Manzoni, she had to swallow an instinct to run as fast as she could in the opposite direction, and instead tried to compose her face into the angelic expression she had seen in the portraits of young Master Twist.

"Wait here, please, Master Twist," said the light porter, pronouncing her name with dubious tones.

Twill stood back as the porter knocked on the door

and entered. From her vantage point, she could see the twin figures of Messrs Farthingale and Shillingsworth sat behind twin mahogany desks. These two men, though they were not related by blood, had spent so many hours of their life together, bent over the same figures, counting the same neat piles of coins, and dreaming the same dreams of pounds, shillings and pence, that they had come to resemble each other as owners sometimes do their dogs. Both were grey-haired, both had a slight stoop of the shoulders, and both had a superabundance of wrinkles, as if they had spent so long buried in ledgers that the lines of figures had become mapped over their faces. Both wore well-cut frock-coats, which hung a little limply off their sloping shoulders, and both had a single monocle – but whereas Mr Farthingale's was gold and hung from a chain around his neck, Mr Shillingsworth's was of tortoiseshell and perched on a small handle, like a pair of opera glasses.

Neither looked up when the light porter entered, but Mr Farthingale – or it might have been Shillingsworth – intoned dryly, "What is it?"

"Sir, I have a young gentleman most urgently requests to see you."

"We are busy," declared Mr Shillingsworth – or was

it Farthingale?

"The young gentleman in question is most insistent," said the porter. "Said you would not object to the intrusion."

"Who is this young gentleman?" said one of the, grey bank managers.

The light porter's answer seemed to have a singular effect on all the inhabitants of the room. "Why, sir, he says his name is – Oliver Twist."

They all swung round to behold Twill, who, taking her cue, now stepped into the room. Mr Bumble let out a wheezing gasp, Madam Manzoni uttered a low bilious moan and Fagin – Fagin stood silent for a moment, his face undergoing several convolutions before settling on a malicious smile.

It was he who recovered first, stepping forward to make low obeisance to "Oliver Twist", taking Twill by the hand and simpering, "Oh, *Oliver*, my dear, dear *boy*, we are so very glad to see you! Ha! Ha! Ha! Delighted. Delighted!"

This reaction – not being quite what Twill expected – rather wrong-footed her.

"Yes, we are *delighted* to see you looking so well," went on the old man, bowing with mock humility. "Why didn't you write, my dear, to say you were coming? We'd have made preparations, indeed we would. Indeed we would."

"I – I did write," said Twill. "I wrote to my guardian – to Mr Brownlow."

"Your humble servants, Master Twist – humble servants," interjected a sweating Mr Bumble, who had levered his giant bulk out of the small chair in which it had been imprisoned and now stepped forward to clasp Twill's hand in his greasy palm, red-faced and puffing like a blowfish. "Indeed, we are honoured to carry out the good work of our maker and of your dear guardian – when he was in his wits, that is," he concluded with a look of pious pity.

"My guardian's work?"

Mr Fagin continued to watch Twill through his thick red eyebrows, with the same curious smile. Madam Manzoni had so far said nothing, but surveyed Twill coolly, her doughy face unreadable.

"Suffer the little children to come unto me," wheezed Mr Bumble with gloriously pompous humility, pumping Twill's hand with excessive enthusiasm. "That is my motto. Since my official pardon and appointment to this auspicious role – by the offices of your guardian, I must say – I have striven to follow the Christian example of that good man Brownlow."

"And what a blessing that you are here to witness your guardian's final act of benevolence, my dear, dear *boy*," said Mr Fagin, with special emphasis on the final word. "Back from the Indies and looking so well when all thought you were lost, my *lad*."

"Yes – um – I came to shore this very morning," said Twill.

"Really?" said Mr Fagin. "On what vessel, may I ask?"

"On the … the – the *Calliope*!" said Twill. "A Merchant Fleet ship."

"I see," said Fagin. "And how did the Indies suit a young *gentleman* like yourself? I am surprised to see you still so pale of skin after your time in the sunnier climes."

"Indeed, I keep out of the sun," said Twill, just as pointedly. "I tend to burn, and I don't believe it is healthy for a child to have skin stained red – or any other colour, for that matter."

"Quite so, quite so!" Fagin gave just the slightest of twitches, but the sinister smile did not leave his face.

"Well, this is most timely, most timely," said Farthingale – or Shillingsworth.

"Indeed, you are present to witness your guardian's

great bequest," said Shillingsworth – or Farthingale.

"Oh, I'm afraid that won't be possible," said Twill, who had just spotted Mr Scapegrace, hitherto hidden from view behind the monstrous presence of Madam Manzoni.

"Won't be possible?" said Mr Bumble, making a choking sound.

"How so, my dear?" said Mr Fagin smoothly.

Madam Manzoni still said nothing, her small beady eyes fixed on Twill with an unreadable expression.

"Because of this document here," said Twill, withdrawing it from inside the pocket of the frock-coat that Dodger had somehow managed to procure her (and which bore all the hallmarks of a Savile Row tailor of the first water), "which grants me full power of attorney over Mr Brownlow's affairs."

There was a collective intake of breath from the assembled company, and a large sniff from the light porter.

"Power of attorney?" said Messrs Shillingsworth and Farthingale in unison.

"When was this granted?" said the former.

"Who witnessed it?" asked the latter.

"I – I … I did," said Mr Scapegrace, stepping out of the shadow of Medora Manzoni – literally and metaphorically for the first time in his life.

"You!" Madam Manzoni's entire bulk quivered, her lumps and layers of flesh like a volcano that might at any moment erupt.

"Y-y-y-es," stammered Mr Scapegrace, shaken by the tremors of her impending explosion but determined to persevere. "A-a-a-and you will see this d-d-document pre-dates Mr Brownlow's bequest – and therefore in-in-invalidates it."

"Invalidates it!" thundered Mr Bumble.

"I-I-I am afraid so," said Mr Scapegrace, continuing with undaunted bravery that made Twill's heart swell with gratitude. "It does."

"So this *boy* has the authority to block his guardian's bequest?" said Fagin, his eyes sparkling dangerously as he spoke. His was a quieter ripple of fury but no less alarming for it.

"Y-y-yes, he d-d-does!" declared Mr Scapegrace, now cowering in anticipation of the impending apocalypse.

"You are saying – do I understand – that the money cannot be handed over?" demanded a blustering Mr Bumble.

"Exactly," said Twill. "Unless…"

"Unless?"

It felt as if everyone in the room were staring at her
– as indeed they were.

"Unless I agree to it."

Chapter 34

*In which many things happen, too numerous to
be summarised here, so you will just have to read on
to find out*

"If my guardian wishes his fortune to be handed over to this philanthropic cause, who am I to prevent it?" said Twill calmly, beginning to enjoy her Oliver role now. "Mr Brownlow desires to make this bequest to the Benevolent Boys' House and the Institute for the Betterment of Young Ladies and I am happy to countersign it." She paused. "But…"

"But?" demanded Mr Bumble, perspiring more heavily than ever.

"But … I have certain conditions."

"Conditions?" said Mr Fagin, raising his extraordinary red eyebrows and apparently not at all discomfited by Twill's advantage in the negotiations.

"Yes, conditions," she went on coolly. "The girl –

Angel – is to be returned to the custody of her friends…"

"Girl?" queried Mr Farthingale – or was it Shillingsworth?

"Angel?" quibbled Mr Shillingsworth – or was it Farthingale?

"No!" ejected Madam Manzoni, quivering like a giant raspberry jelly as she spat forth the single syllable.

"Yes," Twill continued, emboldened. "And Mrs Bumble – née Corney – is to be dismissed from her position in the house of my guardian…"

"Well, I say…" remonstrated Mr Bumble, near to drowning under the deluge of his own perspiration.

"And the boys currently residing in the Benevolent Home are to be released," Twill concluded firmly. "Without further delay. As are the young ladies residing with Madam here."

"Why – well, I…" Mr Bumble wiped his forehead with a large spotted handkerchief, to little effect.

"What temerity!" Madam Manzoni's volcanic flesh quivered red and ablaze.

"And if we meet these conditions you will sign over the entire Brownlow fortune?" said Mr Fagin, eyeing her coolly, like an adder waiting to strike.

"Yes," said Twill. "No questions asked."

There was a long silence. Madam Manzoni quivered.

Mr Bumble dripped. Mr Fagin narrowed his eyes.

"Well, I suppose – given the circumstances – and all things considered…" Mr Bumble blustered damply, turning to his co-conspirators for corroboration and not a little discombobulated by this unexpected turn of events. "That is to say, notwithstanding and without prejudice… We, we might be tempted to accept, mightn't we?"

"I always said you were a sharp *lad*," said Mr Fagin, ignoring Bumble, his gaze focused more intently than ever on Twill. "Didn't I, Oliver, my dear? Didn't I say you were the smartest *boy* I ever encountered? And here you stand before us – just as I predicted … A great young *man*."

"Just as you predicted," said Twill, meeting his dangerous smile with as much coolness as she could muster.

"And you are sure – quite sure – of the legal situation, my dear *boy*?" said Fagin. "I ask only out of concern for you, you understand, my dear."

"Oh, I think you and I understand each other perfectly, Mr Barrabas," said Twill. "And I think we both know that if the game were to be up, it would come out rather worse for you than it would for me – my dear!"

Mr Fagin held her gaze, and Twill could almost see him weighing up the value of Brownlow's fortune versus the satisfaction of revenge. Would he demand his pound of flesh, or take the money and run?

But she was destined never to find out, for at that moment Madam Manzoni arose from her bath chair, wobbling like a colossal blancmange, on feet barely big enough to support her giant bulk, and declared, "This is an impostor! This is *not* Oliver Twist."

The light porter emitted his biggest sniff yet and the twin bank managers ogled with wide-eyed bemusement through their twin monocles.

"An impostor?" said Mr Shillingsworth – or Farthingale.

"Not Oliver Twist?" said Mr Farthingale – or Shillingsworth.

"Not even a boy!" declared Madam Manzoni, her many chins and rolls of flesh undulating like earth tremors. "A girl! And a charlatan, trying to swindle Mr Brownlow out of his fortune! Call the police at once, I say! Have her arrested."

As if at her very command, there came the sound of a commotion outside the room, shouting voices – someone remonstrating, "But – but – you can't go in there. Not to be disturbed…" and a deep low voice Twill didn't recognise, declaring, "Stand back in the name of the law", and then another that she *did* recognise, demanding, "Get out of my way or I'll knock yer block off!"

And then the door burst open and there stood two policemen, top-hatted, brass-buttoned, truncheons in hand ... and behind them, the familiar faces of Baggage, Bob and Dodger.

"What is the meaning of this?" demanded Messrs Shillingsworth and Farthingale in unison.

"We're here with a warrant for the arrest of these persons," declared the taller of the two bobbies, his giant sideburns like two small bushes growing on either side of his face.

"Which persons?" asked the now-very-confused bank managers.

"These persons!" declared Mr Bumble, with a theatrical flourish that sent droplets of sweat raining around the room. "They are common thieves and vagabonds!"

"No – these persons!" said Dodger, who could roister and swagger just as well as Bumble. "They're fraudsters an' swindlers an' they all deserves to be shopped an' scragged!"

"Peachin' to the traps now, young Dodger?" declared

Fagin with a malevolent snarl. "I woutn't have thought it of you, my artful one!"

"Then you really ditn't know me at all, did you, Mr Fagin!" said Dodger, holding his erstwhile mentor's gaze undaunted. "If I can't wring your scrawny old neck meself, I'll make certain sure the fellas at Newgate do it properly this time!"

"Who *are* we supposed to be arresting?" demanded the smaller of the two peelers, who had attempted to grow as fine a pair of sideburns as his counterpart with only partial success, but for which he had compensated by a most elaborately twirled moustache.

"Her! Arrest this girl!" demanded Madam Manzoni, teetering precariously now like the Leaning Tower of Pisa.

"Girl!" said the bewhiskered policeman, who was looking most perplexed by this unaccountable turn of events.

"Yes! She is an impostor, posing as Mr Brownlow's heir."

"Is this true?" asked the moustachioed officer, equally confused.

Twill opened her mouth to answer. For what could she say but yes?

"No!" declared Dodger. "She is not!"

"She most assuredly *is* a girl!" insisted Madam Manzoni, who looked as though she would topple sideways at any moment. "Must we strip her of her breeches to prove it?"

"No!" exclaimed Twill.

"Yes," declared Dodger.

"What?" said Twill, turning to him in horror.

"Yes – she is a girl," Dodger continued. "But she is also Mr Brownlow's heir."

"What?" Twill heard herself demanding for the second time.

Dodger turned from the look of confusion on Twill's face to the furious gaze of Fagin, then to the pale wobbling wrath of Madam Manzoni and finally to the damp, red-faced Mr Bumble.

"*He* knows it well as I," the Artful Dodger declared, nodding towards Bumble. "So does 'is wife if you care to call 'er to bear witness. An' it don't take no high court judge or university pro-fess-or to see she's as alike Oliver as two peas in a green pea pod."

"What exactly are you saying?" said Mr Farthingale, scratching his head in consternation.

"Yes, what exactly is going on?" asked Mr Shillingsworth, mimicking the action of his partner.

"Same year o' birth, same month…" said Dodger.

"An' where did you say you found her, Baggage?"

"Why, on the rubbish heap," said Baggage, stepping forward for the first time, all of a-quiver to find herself addressing two members of the London Constabulary and a room of bigwigs besides. "Down in Mudfog – the old alley behind the workhouse!"

"The same workhouse where Oliver Twist wos born!" said Dodger triumphantly. "Two babies – born a hundred yards from each other the same winter's night, so alike their own guardian can't tell 'em apart. Seems a mighty coincidence if you ask me!"

"What of it!" demanded Fagin, the first to gain his composure. "The power of attorney was granted to Oliver Twist. She is not Oliver Twist."

"A-a-actually, I think you'll find the w-w-wording of the document grants p-p-power of attorney to the child of A-a-agnes Fleming," said Mr Scapegrace, bowing a little apologetically but looking rather pleased with himself. "And this girl is m-m-most assuredly the child of that poor unfortunate young l-l-lady. The r-r-resemblance is quite r-r-remarkable."

"Circumstantial poppycock!" blustered Mr Bumble. "Where's the proof? The proof, I ask you. You want to claim this girl is heir to a fortune. Where's the proof?"

Everyone looked at Twill, but this time it was Baggage

who spoke.

"The twist of paper I gave you – do you still have it?"

Twill looked at her blankly, her mind still madly trying to catch up with the revelations. "I – I do."

"Open it!" said Baggage softly.

"But…"

"Don't matter wha's in there," said that good woman. "You know I'll always be your ma."

"And I'll always be your girl," said Twill, meeting Baggage's loving dishwater eyes as her own threatened to swell over with love and gratitude for the only mother she had ever known.

Then Twill reached for the small kid bag – hardly large enough for a ha'penny bit – that she kept around her neck. She withdrew from it a small package wrapped in a twist of newspaper. Everyone was silent, watching the procedure. Slowly and with trembling fingers Twill withdrew from within the paper a portrait miniature – painted in tiny strokes of watercolour on to ivory and mounted within a tiny golden frame.

Everyone waited for her to speak but she said nothing for a long moment thereafter. She was indeed quite unaware of anyone around her as she stared at the face etched upon the miniature, at the eyes that seemed to look out at her from behind the glass: the same eyes that had gazed on her from the canvas in Mr Brownlow's sickroom. The same eyes she beheld when she looked in a mirror. She caught her breath as the same wave of longing that had overcome her the previous night washed over her again.

Dimly aware of the other occupants in the room peering over her shoulder, and her own heart pounding in her ears, she turned over the miniature and through a haze of tears she deciphered the words engraved thereon: "Agnes Fleming".

"I found it on you that night, in the snow," said Baggage gently. "Hidden among the blanket you wos wrapped in. Is a likeness, I believes – of your mother!"

"My – mother?" Twill's voice sounded distant as if she were listening to it from deep underwater, and she stared at the image with a wave of tenderness.

"This is all very well," said Mr Bumble, blustering through the hushed silence that had fallen upon the assembly with this majestic pronouncement. "But since Oliver Twist is dead, and this preposterous claim remains unproven then Mr Brownlow's bequest still stands!"

"Who says I am dead?"

Chapter 35

*In which another Twist appears in this Tale and
brings it nearly to a conclusion*

Twill was by now quite certain that she must be dreaming. For, standing framed in the doorway, was yet another mirror image of herself – and not in watercolour or oils on canvas or etched on an ivory miniature, but embodied in flesh and blood; a boy with cornflower-blue eyes, hair the colour of gold and a delicacy of features. Instinctively Twill knew that he was the head to her tails, the light to her dark – the other half of her being; a part of herself she had missed all her life without ever realising it was lacking till now.

And behind him, looking a little breathless, stood young Anna Dropsy, the gallant young maidservant who had apprised her beloved master of all the convoluted doings that had led to this moment and brought him to the bank, just in the nick of time.

And it was a curious thing, for the other occupants of the – now very crowded – room had previously been convinced that Twill was the very likeness of her brother. But now Oliver Twist himself stood in the room – for I suppose I need not tell you it was he – the company was impressed not by the similarities between the two but the differences: the subtle distinctions that lay in the light of the eyes, the tilt of the chins, the line of the mouths. Or perhaps it was just something in their general bearing, something indefinable yet incalculably different; a delicacy in the boy, a spark of energy in the girl that made them seem not like two peas in the proverbial pod, but rather like two sides of the same coin, the daybreak to dusk.

And this difference seemed to have the most profound effect upon Mr Fagin.

"Oliver, my dear!" He spoke in a simpering voice now, the dangerous light extinguished from his eyes by the shadow of the gallows that he felt looming over him once more. "Have a little compassion for a confused old man. A dear old friend."

"And, young master Twist," interjected Mr Bumble, who seemed like a pufferfish that had been suddenly deflated, all his oratorical hot air quite extinguished, "was it not I who set you on the path to greatness? Who invented your very name? Who made you Oliver Twist? Why, it was I who lifted you from the den of paupers and put you on the path on which you now tread!"

Oliver Twist beheld them both: the man who had named him, half starved him, sold him, then conspired to rob him of his birthright, and the other, who had kidnapped him, attempted to corrupt him, and kept him from the family and fortune that were rightfully his. He said nothing for a moment. The light of goodness and charity shone out of his face, just as it had done the first day Mr Brownlow beheld it, but it was tempered now with a richer quality, a new maturity that knew the quality of mercy and of justice.

"Arrest them all," he said quietly.

"All?" asked the tall policeman, his whiskers all a-quiver.

"These three." Oliver indicated Bumble, Fagin and Manzoni. "They are fraudsters and swindlers, and the children of London will be safer with them removed from the streets."

Suddenly there was an almighty groan as Madam Manzoni's quivering legs gave way. She swayed for a moment, gurgling most terribly, her eyes rolling in the fantastical puff paste of her face, before her giant bulk came crashing down in the bath chair with such force it seemed to shake the very foundations of the Farthingale and Shillingsworth Bank. Then the terrible sound stopped and she lay slumped in the contraption – white and vast and terrible, with a crooked smile on her face and one little hand hanging limply from its huge arm.

"Somebody call a doctor!" blustered Mr Bumble.

But nobody moved.

"A physician, I say! I feel – I must say, I do declare – I feel most unwell!" Mr Bumble mopped frantically at his brow, stumbling towards the doorway, where the moustachioed officer stopped him in his tracks, producing a giant set of handcuffs that set Bumble perspiring anew.

"A handkerchief, a handkerchief!" Bumble cried, as the chains were locked over his fat little wrists. "My fortune for a handkerchief!"

The onlookers observed this spectacle with stupefied awe and it was Fagin who broke the horrified silence.

"I am an old man," he whispered. "Just an old … old man."

His body seemed to have shrunk and there was terror in the dark eyes beneath the red eyebrows.

Perhaps he was recalling the nights he had spent in the condemned cell at Newgate: the sound of the banging as the workmen assembled the scaffold outside; the hissing cries of the crowd as he passed through the prisoner's grate; the image of those many companions whom he had betrayed hanging limp on the end of the hangman's rope like bundles of old clothes. And the great despair came upon him that he had felt only once before, the despair that had made him rave and bewail his fate like a child or a cornered animal, when he had felt barely human, when he had rocked himself from side to side like a snared beast.

"Oliver, here, here – let me whisper with you!" He seemed desperate, weakened, aged a decade in the same number of minutes.

"I will say a prayer for you," said Oliver, his eyes shining with tears.

"Hang your prayers!" declaimed Fagin, and as the police officers stepped forward to apprehend him he writhed and struggled with the power of desperation and sent up a shriek that rang through the building of Farthingale and Shillingsworth. "Strike you all dead! What right have you to condemn me?"

It was Dodger who looked on him then; Dodger who said simply, "May God forgive this wretched man."

Chapter 36

Chapter The Last

The fortunes of those who have figured in this tale are nearly closed, and what little remains of their history may be simply told. With the return of Oliver, the plot against Mr Brownlow unravelled like a frayed sleeve. How the deception had been practised upon him by the Bumbles. How the apothecary's drugged tea had made his mind captive to their whims. How Mr Fagin had turned his philanthropic enterprise into a den of blackest iniquity for the exploitation of the boys therein. How Madam Manzoni had aided and abetted all this, as well as carrying out her own nefarious activities at the Black Jack. All was brought to light and set before the offices of justice.

The conspirators were duly arrested and taken to

Newgate, though upon their trial it was Oliver himself who petitioned the judge for clemency, asking for their sentences of hanging to be commuted to life sentences of imprisonment. "For even the blackest of sheep deserve the Lord's mercy," the court report recorded him as saying, noting also that when he had begged the judge and jury to "let mercy season justice" his piety and goodness had reduced several onlookers in the gallery – including a certain mealy-mouthed maidservant – to tears.

With the removal of Mrs Corney – and her noxious camomile tea – Mr Brownlow made a remarkable and almost immediate recovery, aided no doubt by his joy in the return of not one but two young wards. Indeed, he took Twill to his bosom as quickly as he had Oliver, bestowing on her all of an adopted father's love and affection, as well as altering his will to bequeath her half his fortune.

Then, with the assistance and guidance of the now *twin* apples of his eye, he set about righting the wrongs brought about during his illness. The Benevolent Home was once more restored to a place of refuge – a home from home where destitute and hungry children might find a warm welcome, a soft bed, a hot meal and the love of a family. I say children, for

Mr Brownlow saw fit to change the name of the institution to "The Twist and Twill Institute for Homeless Boys *and* Girls". He also saw fit to install as house parents one Baggage Jones and her newly wedded husband Bob (who had been so overcome by the tide of recent events he had accidentally proposed to Baggage, who – in a state of equal joy and astonishment – had accepted him).

Most of the blue boys had returned to the home once it had been extensively refurbished, the blacking factory erased from memory and replaced with home comforts and a kitchen large enough for Baggage to whip up cakes by the bakers' dozen. The inky tincture of the blue boys' skin was gradually fading with the weekly system of baths that had been instituted – much to the chagrin of small Nemo, who considered bathing almost as great an abuse as the blacking factory – as well as Baggage's dietary maxim: "Let them eat cake!"

Meanwhile, the Sassy Sisters had also decamped from the printing press to the "Twill 'n' Twist" – as it came to be affectionately known. And soon there came more – more wretched, loveless creatures who crept in from the cold, wet shelter-less midnight streets of London. In shabby rags with bruised and battered souls they came, seeking solace, seeking shelter, seeking a home.

In fact, there were so many orphans now in need of love that Baggage persuaded Mr Brownlow to recruit more mother figures in the shape of the Butterflies – past and present; the beautiful and the faded alike – to care for the loveless children. These dear girls had vast untapped wells of motherly love to give to the little occupants of the Twill 'n' Twist, and so the arrangement worked perfectly, to the mutual satisfaction of all parties.

Baggage had tried to recruit Dodger too, persuading him to take on the role of house leader, but all in vain. Dodger – never one for home and hearth – seemed to have itchier soles to his feet than ever before.

Since he stood in court to watch the closest man he had to a father sentenced to life imprisonment, Mr Jack Dawkins had not been himself. The ducker and diver that had once been the Artful Dodger seemed all cleaned out by the recent turn of events. And, according to Chelsea, no one could bring a smile to his face – not even little Angel, who had been rescued from the clutches of Mrs Spanks by the Sassy Sisters.

Twill longed to talk to Dodger about what was ailing him, but she so rarely saw him these days, a circumstance that caused her more discomfort than she might once have imagined, nor was able to account for.

For Twill herself had been elevated to the life of a young heiress, the stuff of happy endings for most storybook heroines – and yet not so for Twill Brownlow-Jones (she had kept her name, for Twill Twist sounded rather ridiculous, and she considered Baggage as much her family as Oliver and Mr Brownlow). For, while she loved her long-lost brother and her newly found adoptive father, Twill found the necessity of wearing stays, and being subjected to the horrors of curl papers, and drinking tea with other fashionable young ladies … I would say irksome, but that would be to grossly underestimate the abject misery these necessities occasioned for the girl who had grown up running wild on the streets of Camberwell and Denmark Hill, who had risen in the ranks of the Sassy Sisters of Saffron Hill, who had foiled plots, brought villains to justice, freed the oppressed…

The worst of it was she knew she ought to be grateful. She had longed for adventure – and had it not been the best of larks while it lasted? She had longed for family she could call her own – and now she had so much family, with Baggage and Bob, the Butterflies, the Sassy

Sisters, the blue boys, a twin brother and a beloved guardian, that she could barely keep count of them all. Oh, but the old itch gnawed at her so that it was almost impossible to sit still at her embroidery, or keep herself from twitching while at the tea table with the cultured young ladies whose society her guardian wished her to cultivate, but who did not understand her as the Sassy Sisters had, and could not read her very soul the way that Dodger had.

Dodger himself was – unbeknown to her – suffering from a very similar malady, yet his gnawing ache took a more precise shape and form than hers, perhaps indicating that he was the wiser of the two when it came to knowing the name of the dog that had bit him. The streets of London no longer held the thrill they once had for Dodger. His role as Chief Child Protector was redundant now that the Child Catchers had been disbanded and driven from the streets. And he had almost resolved to sail off with his old pal Harry Bates on the *Calliope* – and yet ... something held him back.

And that something bore a distinct resemblance to Miss Twill Jones.

To think of the Artful Dodger himself with a broken heart – pining for a girl no less – was as unthinkable to the young man himself as it may be to the reader, but this was the case, and a very lamentable case it was too.

It was young Oliver who diagnosed the malady in both his dearest sister and best of friends and came up with a cure for both – though implementing the remedy caused him the bitterest heartache of his young and not always easy life.

One morning he and his new sister were sitting in the parlour, he reading a book of Mr Keats's poetry, she stabbing angrily at a sampler of embroidery that was already pock-marked with unpicked stitches and the violence of her needle, when there was a rap at the door.

"I wonder who that could be?" said young Oliver, with a look in his eye that suggested he knew exactly who the caller was (hardly surprising since he had summoned him there by messenger not two hours earlier).

The butler rapped on the door and ushered in the guest. "Mr Jack Dawkins to see you, sir – miss."

"Dodger?" said Twill, looking up in surprise, her face heating up unexpectedly.

Her erstwhile pickpocketing companion had grown a little in the months since we saw him in Farthingale and Shillingsworth Bank – as boys of that age are wont to do – and he had a smattering of down on his upper lip that gave him a distinctly grown-up appearance and which set Twill's stomach into a state of disorder, the reason for which she could not fathom.

"Miss Brownlow-Jones," said Dodger, bowing low but failing to meet her eye.

This greeting had the effect of worsening her symptoms rather than curing them, and fortunately Oliver broke the awkward silence.

"Jack here tells me he wishes to join the Merchant Fleet."

"What?" said Twill. "But ... you can't!"

"Why can't I?" demanded Dodger, eyes shooting up to meet hers now.

"Because – well, because..." Twill's stomach symptoms seemed to have extended to her heart, which was hammering wildly. "It's too dangerous!"

"Dangerous, pah!" said Dodger. "When did you get so lily-livered, Camberwell?"

"I'm as brave as you and braver, and you know it!" said Twill, forgetting in a moment all the ladylike manners that Mr Brownlow had been attempting to instil in her. "And don't call me Camberwell!"

She glared at him so horribly that a lesser young man might have withered or turned to stone beneath her stare. Not so Dodger, who stared back just as ferociously.

"Indeed you are, my sister," said Oliver, intervening before either did a damage by the savagery of their glares. "Which is why Mr Brownlow needs you."

Twill turned to him, only half hearing what he was saying, the other half of her brain unaccountably fixated on the presence of Master Dawkins – his annoyingly broad chest … and blazing angry eyes … and the irritating shape of his freckled nose.

"The Brownlow estates in the Indies are in quite a state," Oliver went on. "My guardian needs someone to go and oversee them – and to make a stand against the slave trade once and for all. And he has suggested that you, my dear Twill, would be just the woman."

"Me go to the Indies?" Twill's astonishment was amplified by Dodger's alarm.

"It's no place for the lily-livered," Oliver went on. "The life over there didn't suit me one bit. What with pirates and slavers, and sea creatures that you only hear of in fairy tales…"

Twill and Dodger were both staring at him.

"Pirates?" said she.

"Sea creatures?" asked he.

"Oh, there are adventures enough to be had over there to keep you busy for a lifetime," said Oliver, who at this moment was showing his truest wellspring of goodness. He had never had a sister, and his tender heart had attached itself to hers from the very first moment they met, so that she was now essential to his happiness. Yet he saw that adventure was essential to hers. And so perhaps was Jack Dawkins.

"And, Dodger, I would like you to go too," said Oliver, adding, because he was only human after all – and fully aware of the effect his next words would have – "to look after her."

"I don't need anyone to look after me!" declared a furious Twill.

"Be that as it may," said Oliver, trying not to smile. "I'd sleep easier if I knew Jack was with you."

Twill looked at Dodger. Dodger looked at Twill. Neither said a word. He gave a sniff. She wrinkled her nose and shrugged. That was all. But that was all that needed to be said. For now.

"I – I'm not sure I'm fit to run a big estate," said Twill, turning back to Oliver. "I can't seem to even pour the tea properly. Or sew cross-stitch. Or dance a quadrille…"

"Nobody cares over there whether you are born a lady or brought up in a pigsty," said Oliver. "The New World cares less about such silly distinctions than the old. It's a place of strange winds, magical shifting sands

255

– a place where any man can make a fortune on his wits. Or any girl too, for that matter."

"Oh, but how I will miss you all!" said Twill, clasping the hand of her brother, whom she had come to love as she did the air of London's streets, as she did Baggage.

"We'll come back and visit," said Jack, deciding this was the moment for him to take charge, before Twill got caught up in the soppy stuff. "When I have made my fortune I will probably want to come back and purchase one of them new mansions wot they're building up in Mary-Le-Bone. Or perhaps a country shootin' box, or a place in Brighton or Bath – though if Bath's not good enough for our young queen, maybe it's not good enough for Dodger neither!"

Twill looked at him with an expression of mingled irritation and amusement. "You won't last two minutes out there without me, Jack Dawkins. All them sea monsters and marauding pirates – yup, you're gonna need a girl to protect you!"

"A girl!"

"Yes!" declared Twill. "This girl!"

And so that is where the story ends, with wrongdoers punished, benevolence rewarded, Twill and Dodger setting sail for a life of roaming adventure, and the righting of worldwide wrong. And what of equality for the female of the species? An equal chance for the girls who were so maligned when our tale began? Well, it may not be fully achieved – for we should not forget that women will not to get to vote for over half a century beyond the conclusion of this tale! – but let us say the female fight-back has begun – and our heroine is throwing the first punch.

Acknowledgements

My first encounter with Dickens was when my big sister was studying *Great Expectations* for O Level and started calling our little brother "Mr Pumblechook". There was something about that glorious name, and all those others – Magwitch, Jaggers, Pip Pirrip, Orlick, Wopsle and the Aged P – that made my brain pop and fizz! But then I auditioned unsuccessfully for the school production of *Oliver!* and got the hump with Dickens for a while, so the first Dickens I actually read was *Bleak House* at S Level (no, that's not a typo – S Level was a thing back in my day!). It was the first time I had ever seen a teacher cry – the wonderful Mr Jennifer Barratt weeping over the death of Jo in a portacabin at Lymm High School on a rainy November morning in 1990 made a deep impression on me. I was studying Nineteenth Century History at the time and I started to see that Dickens' books were more than brilliantly woven plots and wonderful, eccentric characters – he was also a social campaigner who used stories to fight against social ills, boldly and imaginatively campaigning to improve the lives of the most desperate and overlooked in society through his fiction. That those powerful messages continued to resonate across the decades, across the centuries – enough to make my teacher cry over the death of a homeless boy who was a figment of a genius's imagination – had a profound effect on me, and fundamentally shaped the writer, and the teacher, I have always tried to be.

As a student at St Hugh's College, Oxford in the early '90s, I had the privilege to attend lectures by John Carey and Kathleen Tillotson, where I was introduced more widely to the wonders of Dickens' canon. It was my tutor, the brilliant Dr Isobel Rivers, who first said to me, "To understand Dickens, you have to understand the Blacking Factory". She made me see that the terrified young boy who had been forced to work in a factory when his father was thrown into debtor's prison is present in all of Dickens' fiction. He is also at the very heart of *Another Twist in the Tale* – he is the germ from which this story began. The tragedy that thousands of such children exist around the world today, working in sweatshops, many in conditions of modern slavery, is something I hope the book might make young readers think about.

Over the years I have had the privilege to teach Dickens to dozens (possibly hundreds?) of amazing pupils – largely *Great Expectations* but latterly *Bleak House* and *Hard Times*. I'm not going to lie, Dickens can be a hard sell at GCSE. At first, the language can seem impenetrable, the plots confusing and convoluted (examiners might like to think whether *Hard Times* is really a novel calculated to foster a life-long love of Dickens in 15 year olds!). But – oh, we had a lot of fun along the way, and I like to think that all my lovely pupils past and present came – eventually (begrudgingly?) – to a love of Dickens' brilliance (or – in the case of my current GCSE group – that you might do so when these pesky exams are over – Good Luck, my wonderful ones!). So, this book is a big thank you to you all – you have all inspired me, made me laugh, made me think, made me see things anew and afresh and through the lens of different generations – and this book is dedicated to you! They were Hard Times but they were ever the Best of Times, eh kids!

It is also dedicated to the members of the King Edward's School Creative Writing Society, where the idea for this novel popped into my head whilst we were writing stories inspired by Carol Ann Duffy's *The World's Wife*. Especial thanks to Netta Claydon, who switched the lightbulb in my head with a passing comment (and who is, and always was, a far greater writer than I can ever hope to be!). I am also hugely grateful to Anna Winkelmann, my first reader and (second!) best editor, whose input was so invaluable I named a character in her honour, for though she is definitely NOT "mealy-mouthed and sour-looking", she is possessed of the same imagination and heroism as her name-sake! Thank you to all the young writers of CWS, past and present – you keep me on my toes as I try to keep up with your brilliance!

I owe a huge debt to the colleagues I have had the privilege to work with over the years in the English and Drama Departments of Haberdashers' Aske's School for Girls, Francis Holland Girls' School, St Paul's Girl's School and King Edward's School, Bath, who have inspired and challenged me and whose intellectual companionship and inspiring example has immeasurably enriched my writing – but also my life.

I am so grateful to the various academics and

institutions who helped me with this novel: to Philip Thorne, editor of the utterly invaluable Penguin Classic edition (I fell a little in love with your appendices!); Dr Paul Schlicke, editor of *The Oxford Companion to Charles Dickens*; Professor Michael Slater; Dr Sara Malton; Elizabeth Velluet and Dr Tony William (The Dickens Fellowship); Lee Jackson, author of *Walking Dickens' London*; the staff and curators of the Charles Dickens Museum; and the amazing Ben from the *Twists and Turns: The Places that Inspired Oliver Twist* Walking Tour (www.benscitytours.com) who took me in the footsteps of young Oliver and brought Dickensian London to life. I am hoping that Dickens scholars the world over will forgive any deviations from Dickens' original, and that you will take them in the spirit of Dickensian playful inventiveness in which they are intended. I also hope you will appreciate my attempt to translate the energy of Dickens' prose style and the gloriousness of his language for a younger audience. I didn't want to dumb-down for them, but I did want to make it accessible enough to make them want to pick up one of the originals. I like to think that Mr Dickens himself, if he has been watching over my enterprise, will have done so with a wry smile of amusement, occasional chuckles at my temerity, and knowing that this is very much a homage to his work – a 'gateway to Dickens' which I hope may be the first step on a magical reading journey for many young bookworms.

And it's not only characters from *Oliver Twist* who find their way into this tale! Eagle-eyed book lovers might catch a glimpse of Bitzer, a certain Edith Wharton matriarch (dedicated with love to my KES sixth formers, past and present), as well as lines from Shakespeare, Webster and many more. Oh, and I could never have written this book without Georgette Heyer, who was my "gateway to the classics", thanks to the staff of Lymm Library, who handed an eleven-year-old me a copy of *Arabella* and introduced me to the world of gleaming hessians, sprig muslin, and gaming hells. From there it really is just a short hop to Austen, Eliot and the Brontës, so Georgette was my stepping stone – and still remains my favourite guilty-reading pleasure!

As always I am hugely indebted to my wonderful agent Caroline Montgomery, whose insight, wisdom and friendship I value so dearly, and to everyone at Nosy Crow, particularly my amazing editor Tom Bonnick, who is wise, wonderful, bold and brilliant!

But most of all to my wonderful family – wide and small, inlaws and outlaws – especially Jonny, Joe and Elsie (who actually reads my books and whose impeccable taste I defer to in all matters!). Thanks for putting up with me, and I love you all!